THIS WICKED TONGUE

Also by Elise Levine

Blue Field
Requests and Dedications
Driving Men Mad

This Wicked Tongue

stories

Elise Levine

A JOHN METCALF BOOK

BIBLIOASIS
WINDSOR, ONTARIO

FIRST EDITION

Levine, Elise, author
This wicked tongue / Elise Levine.

Short stories.
Issued in print and electronic formats.
ISBN 978-1-77196-279-7 (softcover).--ISBN 978-1-77196-280-3 (ebook)

I. Title.

PS8573.E9647T55 2019 C813'.54 C2018-904446-2
C2018-904447-0

Edited by John Metcalf
Copy-edited by James Grainger
Typeset by Chris Andrechek
Cover designed by Natalie Olsen

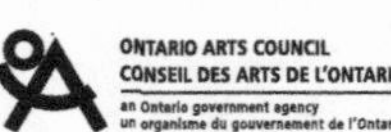

Published with the generous assistance of the Canada Council for the Arts, which last year invested $153 million to bring the arts to Canadians throughout the country, and the financial support of the Government of Canada. Biblioasis also acknowledges the support of the Ontario Arts Council (OAC), an agency of the Government of Ontario, which last year funded 1,709 individual artists and 1,078 organizations in 204 communities across Ontario, for a total of $52.1 million, and the contribution of the Government of Ontario through the Ontario Book Publishing Tax Credit and Ontario Creates.

PRINTED AND BOUND IN CANADA

For DS

And then we sang! And then we sang!
—Shirley Jackson,
We Have Always Lived in the Castle

CONTENTS

Money's Honey

If I moved my head, the air turned dark and blurred my breathing and I felt sick, bad sick.

It was the middle of the day in the middle of July, mid-desert. If we ran the AC, the car overheated. If we drove over sixty, the car overheated.

Are you drinking enough? he said. I told you, keep drinking.

I couldn't—the water hot as tar. I gave myself up. Whatever happens, I said silently, careful not to move my lips. Believe I'm yours.

But I faced forward to behold the black and white in front of me. What a world. It was like the heat gave me X-ray vision. A bus breached past, air-conditioned—I could tell because the windows looked sealed and inside people chatted and played cards, ignoring the nothing outside. Twenty minutes later we passed the bus pulled over on the interstate shoulder, engine smoking, suckahs. We snailed on until a stray palm snaked into view—better believe I kept my eyes open—and then an exit, Indio, a gas station where we could fill up and a café where we could eat.

Partway through my burrito I wobbled to the bathroom, thinking I should after all this time. No pee came. My underwear, stretched between my knees, webbed with lines of salt. So much in me.

I flushed though I didn't have to and struggled to do myself back up. I splashed water on my face. I opened the door to the tiny bathroom. The café wasn't like what I thought a café should be, candles on the tables and music playing, him facing me.

I moved nearer. His plate lay at his elbow, and by his lowered head and bobbing shoulders it seemed he'd started on mine. Mr. Skinny. I never knew where he put it—bags of corn chips and plastic-wrapped hot dogs and subs, jewel-boxed Krispies washed down with Supersizees, and starting in Oklahoma the biscuits and gravy at Mickey Dee's. And still his bones left bruises on me each time we joined our hearts together. Always hungry. His thin brown hair matted to his head, sticking up in places like he'd slept in a ditch for a year. The rest of him a scarecrow fixed to poles. Or a scrap of torn plastic bag flapping in a field—I wondered was it ever filled with something, who it used to belong to.

But I loved him, yeah. I felt baggy myself from the drive, my skin too big and stretched over me like a waste of plastic wrap. And that blur so near it felt like any which way.

Dizzy and ditzy are not the same thing. I believe in signs and in knowing what I know despite what anybody tells me. Stubborn bitch, you're so stupid. Or, Dummy. And those aren't the worse.

Mostly I lay in the back all the way here, at first sleeping or pretending to, and then with my eyes staring at all I'd never seen before and not ashamed to admit it, once we were a long way from Ontari-ari-ari-o. So much sky, each moment different. When I sat, green hills, sands like the sea. He drove far into the night and I'd wake to pink licking the windows like a thousand wet puppies. I'd manage him apart from me and let myself out. Fog welling in the ditches. I'd walk a few steps and the haze would lift, as if I'd squeezed my last tears and could get on with things. Like a rest stop with clean bathrooms. Truck rigs neatly lined up. Men mostly, asleep. I never felt so safe. When I'd come back to the car and open the door, on my side there'd be food piled from the stash in the trunk, chips and chocolate bars grabbed in quick handfuls, whatever was most convenient at each station while I'd slept, only waking to the gunning engine and the over-lit midnight stores blown behind us like nuclear blooms in old movies. And then the grainy aftermaths of night forests, local roads.

In Indio, in a café where no music played, he chewed the burrito as if afraid it might escape. His shoulder blades were thin moons.

What could I say to draw him to me, or me to him? Most of the time words don't mean a thing. They twist mean and not much to do with the truth.

So I closed my eyes to make our closeness more real. And that's when I knew—later there would be Nevada. And later, sure enough, I played a slot at a stop near Reno, lost someone else's fifty cents.

And I knew that before near-Reno I would leave my burner behind in a burger shop bathroom. Just in case. I knew I would shut my eyes to Hollywood and Vine, and when I woke behold a blue-powder PCH heaven pressed to my skin.

In the café in Indio, I took a step blind, then opened my eyes. He'd finished eating and pushed away my plate too.

And oh, his hair was dark and long.

He is someone I left behind. Terrible to say. But knowing it, my scalp tickles, my knees plump.

My shit is together. I'm coming home.

This one's Rudolph or Dieter. Maybe Sheck? Definitely weird.

I get ice at the next gas station while he pays. He shoots me a look like he can't believe his kingdom of lost lambs and charity is ending here and now with a roll-over skid into the bang-wall of my ingratitude. For I am a prison unto myself.

You want that too? the cashier asks him.

I slug the five-pounder down on the counter and the boy punches the numbers in. But no, Sheck whatever has to make an issue, patting the left pocket of his yellow windbreaker. Just put my wallet away, he whines.

He blinks several times, trying to hold his ground. Which to me makes no difference. His eyes are like candles that have already gone out.

We get back in the car. I dandle the bag on my lap. He drives us onto the interstate again, then gets off at the next exit which has lodging, and checks us in.

He sits on the one chair in our room. I lie on the bed, crack cubes between my teeth to keep the nausea down.

Shut up, he says, I can't hear myself think.

A guy who likes to hear himself think. I guess that's what he's doing now in the shower.

Yay me—with the water running so loud, I've got the TV on, sound tamped so he won't know. I don't mind not hearing what people say.

I spread dinner on the bed. I like orange crackers the most. Next, popcorn. Then anything salty, or sweet-sour—mac 'n cheese, peanut brittle, lime taffy enough for two. As for beer, I secretly prefer Michelob Light but if asked I say Bud, their commercials are so cool. When I have my boy that's what I'll call him.

Fat girl, some call me. Hey there, fat slut.

Like I'm there just to get a load of them. What they don't know is, I'm saving, one bill at a time. No one notices, their attention always somewhere I'm not.

The water shuts off. This one comes out of the bathroom wearing a towel, eyes gray and serious like there are no good memories to fill them—all there is to notice about him. Plus that he belongs to some church.

He starts with it. Didn't the lord deliver Daniel? Mr. Moody Voice sings into the motel ceiling. Didn't the, didn't the, Loord?

I'm still cramming food like there's no tomorrow and he gives me a look then catches himself, gives it a rest. Ever since yesterday morning at the Utah line he knows what's coming—things he can't help but like.

He can't help himself with the singing though. Join me, he bids, holding his pale arms out so his towel slips to the carpet. Stand with me lovely bride and drop your jaw, lift your palate. Let Jesus hear you love him. Remember Lord is a long-held note.

He taps his hairless chest where his heart might be. Listen for him here, he says.

The next morning we sleep late, creamy dreamy. He showers again while I sneak-watch TV. Later at a service center he buys me a snow globe with salt-sprayed mountains. Then I sleep and wake at a truck stop in Wyoming, order anything I want off the menu, tater tots and an ostrich burger, ketchup, no onions.

The waitress is old. She smiles and her wrinkled face resembles fork-tender pastry. First time? she asks and I smile as shyly as I can.

Back in the car I can't stop thinking. Wasn't she the nicest thing? Wasn't she?

He rolls his eyes upward as if he's forgotten he's driving. Makes me nervous. Lord Jesus help me, he says, shaking his head and gazing at the road again as if Jesus has instructed him to do so.

Thank you, Jesus, I think and don't say.

Shut up with it already, he says anyway, fingers clenched on the steering wheel. You're so stupid you ought to put a lid.

I make a point of not answering though he probably won't notice, he's now so intent on hands at two and ten, making time as darkness grows. We're making good time, he says, like I don't already know, then he points to a highway sign that looks like a deer in headlights. Nebraska, he says. Brasker and then Chicago. Shy-town, get it?

And after a while I do.

Took you long enough, he says.

The lights of passing cars roll off me like drops of water. The windshield streams. I speed in bubbles of near sleep and when I fully wake, Iowa, morning, eggs and waffles at a truck stop called The Deck. I'm a bit ripe but not too bad, a sour smell rising from my thighs, the backs of which are plastered to the booth seat while he cuts his Denver with the edge of his fork and double-doubles his coffee. I wait until he's halfway through to make a second round of the buffet. Crunchy hash browns, sausages and bacon, chunks of cantaloupe and watermelon in heavy syrup, and the line of customers waiting to be seated, and a woman saying, Chi-cah-go, it's-my-kind-of-town, in a way that sounds like something she's heard before. Like it means something. She hoots and several other women honk in. Behind them, beyond the large window, there's a giant sign with a picture of playing cards. Beneath the sign, giant rigs sit neatly cut and shuffled across the monster lot.

I sit back down with my brimming plate.

Looks like we got here at the right time, he says.

I drizzle syrup over my bacon. I butter my toast. Judging by the brochures arranged in wire racks near the front of the restaurant we're near the Quad Cities. But before or after, and what does Quad mean? I mean, four I know, I wasn't born yesterday contrary to popular opinion, but what's figured in? I pick at a piece of burnt potato, bite my lip to taste blood. And the supreme creator of Mr. Choir Director's church lives downstate Illinois and apparently wants me to go too, and why?

No matter what happens, no way will I ask.

The waitress who pays me no mind slaps the check down in front of him—before I've finished—and he slides out of the booth. Sit tight, he tells me. In all seriousness this might take a while, would you believe I've been stopped up for days?

Three drops of Tabasco on my spoon.

He chuckles. I suggest you make yourself right at home, he says.

I chuckle right back. And when he's gone I leave the check on the table and pad through the restaurant. Outside, I turn the handles on the gum-ball machine, wish I had a quarter. I recheck the folded-over bills in my jeans pockets. It's not raining but it feels like it might.

An old couple says, Morning, morning. Looks like rain, don't it, don't it just?

Retirees, dollars to doughnuts. They've got a hunch-backed Bichon with a floppy red bow in her frizzy white hair. She suddenly zings toward me, pretty fast for an old girl.

Missy, Missy! the couple calls at once in a mock mad that Missy ignores.

I kneel, let her lick my face—a good sour.

Say how do you do, Missy, the man and woman warble over each other. How do you do?

Still on my knees, deep breath, I don't say it but I see it—for starters, my poor boobies are so squashed by my too-small bra that I'm crawling inside like I'm getting ready to take the first steps out of my mind, like Miss Missy here doo-dahing in circles around me, how cute.

I stand. But my too-tight jeans remind me even more and I try to smooth them down below my hips. Which reminds me at least my money is there.

So I kneel again. And bless her, the dog licks my hands and her tongue is like lightning and soft rain, a shower of coins. Rain that's to come, only better.

I close my eyes and it happens again—only this time there's more. A cloud drops off I-80 and sails over, and I suddenly know how to play the hand I've been dealt, a blur that's not darkness blotting things but a brightness so fast I can't slow it down.

It'll be, Are you hungry, child? Are you tired and thirsty? While the gray man in the bathroom fumbles to open himself and in my mind I draw a blind against him. The couple and Missy will live somewhere like Bumfuck, Michigan, where they'll put me on the International, the train that takes me home.

My spirit fills me, dips and doodles like laundry on a line.

When I get there, Daddy will call my boy Little Man. And all will be forgiven—all my ways. There'll be pink store-bought cakes for birthdays, butter-brickle ice cream. Rides on a pony called Pickles.

Buddy boy, I'll say one day. We'll be sitting on the steps leading to the kitchen door, his grampie crouched in the drive, attaching streamers to the handlebars of a training bike. It'll have a banana seat with sparkles underneath the plastic see-through. I can just see my little guy big-wheeling around.

I'll lean over, hold him close, press his ears to his little head. Float lines from Snoop Dogg like a charm over his Ritalin dreams. Who's Mummy's boy? I'll whisper, pull his leg to get him going. Let him wonder who loves who.

The Riddles of Aramaic

Your life is in my hands, Em usually thinks—and a green surge, voltaic, jams her jock's tight gut. When she leans closer over the pale and weak, laid out inertly in test tubes of hospital beds, a bug-zapper sound commands her cochlea. She knows no one else can hear it. It is her privilege.

Stay with me, the loved ones shrill, rent with panic at the thought of being left behind. Some make clawing motions at their throats.

They look like birds—hollow where they should be solid, entirely crushable. Others bellow at the soon-to-expire like pricked bulls.

Don't go.

Not Em. She apprises the curdled skin and damp kitten sighs, brows furrowed with suffering. Go, is what she thinks. Let me help you. I am blessed.

This morning she feels irritable. A black mood jimmies her veins, equal parts guilt, shame, desire—the tumblers of a lock tidying into place.

The patient—a man only recently delivered by Team Oncology into an awareness of his metastasizing condition—blinks at the acoustic-tile ceiling like a newborn. Opposite Em, his wife strokes his arm, calmly gazing at him as she sits in her chair with unfussy composure. Today she is a neat package, fancy pants creased, pale-blue driving mocs the colour of her eyes. Hair expertly highlighted, warm copper graining rich mahogany.

Yesterday she'd undone. Head down, neck jutted forward, she charged up to Em's table in the cafeteria, despite only having met her the previous afternoon and clearly oblivious of how Em had pushed for this first date over thin coffee with the ENT.

Tell me, the woman honked. You're the expert. What am I supposed to say to our friends? Sorry, can't do dinner Saturday, Ken'll be dead by then?

Two months into her residency in clinical pastoral education, Em has grown certain of one thing. Grief makes people greedy, selfish as insects. She stared back at the creature whose name, Em only then recalled, was Marta. Her face was bloated, almost engorged. Like a tick.

The doctor—knee-jiggling perfectionist handsome with high forehead and narrow wrists, high strung, twice married—recoiled fastidiously, excused himself and fled.

Em felt a spray of annoyance at the top of her head, crystals glittering into the bucket of spite one at a time. Ken, she thought. Right, the patient's name is Ken and he's going fast. She allowed a cruel micro-smile to laminate her lips, and settled in for the show. Soon the gestures would trip across Marta's visage, the visible spasms of the snakes and ladders of inner reckonings. Self-recrimination, incendiary hopeless rage, despair—self-justification if she were lucky or insensate or both. In anticipation Em pushed back her paper cup and danced her fingertips on the table top.

But Marta flicked straight, her expression blade bright as if she'd just discovered she could strip to the pith of the thing—she would be a widow shortly, but for the moment that was inconsequent, because she had her enemy now. She looked almost happy with the knowledge.

Em had run yesterday evening to shake the scene. Humility, mortification, forgiveness. Counting street lamps, cars, her breath between this curb and that—a counter, she'd count the bats slopping through the heliotrope twilight if she could be sure of each smudged shape—she peeled off a sixteen-miler, seven-fifty pace, her marathon tempo, cycling through to a serviceable redemption, flanked by night as she stretched. She hadn't behaved that badly, had she?

Today she's really paying—pain, Ibuprofen galore, CBD oil in moderation. She cautiously stretches her legs in front of her while behind her the sheers covering the windows gasp in the hospital's air system. Her left Achilles is hot. A cranky yawn stalks her throat and blooms like a weed in the back of her mouth. Her jaw pops suppressing it.

Behind her, Em hears the squish of a nurse's shoes, the occasional brusque clog of a surgeon making the rounds for the routine checking of fresh incisions. Sequestered here in this private room, the footsteps cause her to feel even younger than she is—in this world but not of it. Cribbed while the crackerjack adults make haste and lay waste around her, busy with their ancient bustling pathways. She feels drained, absorbed against her will by a familiar, tedious longing to be swept up.

She's missed out on something. Personal suffering, for instance—her own. Its absence is an itch she can't locate, crawling uselessly around her scalp. Studying hard, paying for a portion of her way through divinity school by temping part time in the registrar's office, inwardly searching (wrestling with psyche-shredding doubts would be overstating the case) before becoming certain that her calling is to facilitate the delicate transmissions between the dying and the living—all in the service of her effort to compensate.

With Ken and Marta, Em recognizes an intimacy from which she's excluded, a circuit from which she is barred. The effect is hypnotic, evokes in her a stale yearning. She forms a mental picture of half-gnawed graham crackers scattered around the base of a milk-stained glass, detects emerging into the bottom of the frame two tiny child fists, her own, while an enclosing cyclorama revolves clockwise and she feels—she's not sure what. Returned or something. Unworthy. Verry verry sleepy.

She steals a glance at the wall clock above the door, then Marta, who startles. Though she's been stealth-watching Em, the woman's eyes are soft and light rinsed. She's the very picture of unravaged, defiant serenity. Verry obnoxious.

Ken and Marta, Marta and Ken. Brushing her teeth that night, Em worries the couple around in her head. Two weeks ago he'd looked in the mirror while shaving and suddenly crumpled over as his spine gave, bone against bone corrading to dust the first sign of illness, what a shocker. Now he's going faster than medicine can prevent let alone predict. Which is like what? Em thinks. She scrubs her mouth and pictures Einstein mirror-gazing and thinking of eternity. Then another image comes to her. A man in racing shorts and tank trying to outpace death, wings of ash lathering from his athletic shoes to indicate impotent speed. There, success. Ken does make Em feel spiritual. Visionary almost. He's like a crystal ball she can gaze into and see anything she wants.

Or would if it weren't for Marta. Brushing an invisible crumb from Ken's shoulder, smoothing his brow, caressing his earlobe. Picking at and preening him. Thirsty? she keeps asking and he keeps smiling. Putting aside Marta's outburst yesterday, their bliss is as implacable as a butter dish. And serves as a wedge between Em and her meditations. Hard to intuit imperfections, pulled threads, wrinkles, handholds for her journey into elevated realms from which she might contemplate humankind's dark wormy soul—harrowed, harried, embittered at finding itself not long for this world. Never long enough.

She can't work like this. What else is she supposed to get out of it all without that vertiginous short-cut to god? That non-denominational, non-anthropomorphic, non-culturally determined cynosure of holiness, since Em is progressive and unfettered. Was profiled last year along with several other maverick pastors-in-training in a sleek, large urban center magazine, which dubbed them The New Ecumenicals.

Sometimes she thinks of other places in the world she might minister. Maybe when she graduates. Help refugees from torture, rape, and any of the other multi-purpose abuses that despots and poverty breed. But then she thinks if she just works a little harder she can get what she needs here, now. The tough stuff? Maybe later, much.

She spits into the sink, tries imagining man and wife's couplings. Tender, mutually respectful is as far as Em can penetrate—she's distracted by the sounds of her mother and father in the den next door, their TV on, the murmur of their voices rising and falling above the shush of running water. The clink of ice in their nightly glasses of diet ginger ale—her nice old parents, it's as if they're pickled in it.

She turns off the tap, leans forward and rests her elbows on the countertop and shields her head with her palms. Hello, inertia.

Greetings from the Northwoods! ☺

So she texts her friends, but the missives are becoming increasingly less frequent and sincere. When she'd applied to do her residency in this small city in which she'd grown up—the cheapest alternative by far, four months rent-free living with ma 'n pa—she'd convinced herself of early morning runs on dew-aquiver forest trails and sunsets blushing off the lake on her post-work rambles past her old nostalgia-soaked haunts. On her days off, barbecues on the patio, platters of grilled corn she'd pick and shuck herself, the neighbours' seven-year-old twins tripping through the sprinkler on her parents' lawn, stubbed toes, crying. Em proffering comfort like frosty tumblers of lemonade.

It would be so—she can't remember *what* she'd thought as she finished her term papers, plowed through her finals, aced her Greek and Latin exams.

In the bathroom she doffs her self-made skullcap, places her chin on her overlaced knuckles, and meets her own image. Dusting of freckles over fine-pored alabaster skin. Clara-bow mouth. Lucid gray eyes. She is pretty and smart. In the fall she will solve the riddles of Aramaic. ☺ Somehow, though, she'd allowed herself to forget what it is like to endure this house, where one always knows who is in the room next door and the one next to that—a comfy dwelling with the kind of domestic overcrowding endemic to a middle class that's almost extinct, the place resembling a tableau vivant behind dusty glass she might pass without a second glance in a museum. ☹

She tries, she does. I did not have a loving family, she mouths in hopes of convincing the mirror. I *have* suffered.

An untruth. She'd had an ordinary upbringing. Cupcakes and sparklers and the photo albums to prove it.

A wavering image alights her head. A tinfoil tiara, rainbow cuff of candles. The dining room chock-a-block with children singing. More tinfoil—hidden treasure in the cake, to be gleefully forked into and discovered to mighty chortles and snorts at Em's ninth birthday party. The day before, her mother had scooped nickels, dimes, and quarters and washed them, then painstakingly wrapped each coin in a pocket of aluminum and dropped them into the batter, stirring well to distribute them evenly—she was the type of woman who couldn't bear to see even one child go without. It was amazing no one's little Judy or Jeff had choked to death as they pigged through a second or third chocolatey slice.

Make a wish, Em! And she'd huffed and she'd puffed and she'd blown the house down.

Her child self had just had her first revelation. That she would like to hate her foolish mother. Too bad mater's behaviour hadn't been less pardonable.

Ever since, if Em concentrates too intensely on what she wants, a tiny glowing disc kaleidoscopes an inch away from her forehead and her temples throb. She has to lie down for nauseated hours in a darkened room.

She shrugs at her reflection, combs her hair, puts the toilet seat down, and sits to don her lace-up ankle braces. The braces help keep the tendons along the bottom of her feet—inflamed through overuse—stretched during the night. The goal is to prevent the scar tissue—which forms around the plantar fascia if she sleeps naturally, with her feet in a foreshortened position, toes pointed down—from shattering when she steps out of bed in the morning. She twists her mouth to the side and makes a sound like glass breaking. As quietly as she can, she makes another noise mimicking the noise she makes when the scar tissue unpieces.

Ay yi yi. Her body is a Rolodex of pain. Bone spurs. Damaged illio-tibial band, unstable patellar meniscus. Last year, just when she was ramping up her mileage in preparation for the fall marathon, a disabling, near-demoralizing stress fracture in her hip. Oy. Pressure building and ebbing like a lava lamp in her sphincter the past six months. The worst thing—when she scratches herself she can't find the sweet spot and wakes with welts on her neck, legs, and back. Something about the way her nerves are bundled. Oddly, not like most people's.

She leaves the bathroom and hobbles to her bedroom. On her pillow a stuffed Eeyore, disheveled and grumpy, one-eyed ever since she'd poked him with a stick when she was six for no reason she would ever remember. Pennants above the neatly made bed from high school races, college track and field team. The cheerful coverlet, dresser drawers full of properly organized garments. Everything here saps her.

Why are you moping? her mother and father would ask her when she was ten, eleven, fourteen.

They'd look concerned—brows furrowed, mouths tugged down at the corners. What one would expect.

I'm not moping, she'd say. I'm practicing moping.

Her kindly confused parents would wander off, befuddled. It sickened her to watch them. There was nothing they could do to surprise her. She could have killed them for that.

Ever since her summer-camp days—when murky heat and cicadas chanting combined with rapid-onset pubescence to create an intuition of ambitiously mystical escalations, ascendancies—she has wanted to make something of herself. And in doing so, the world. It is her struggle. She is a project she can perfect. A prize she must win.

As for her feelings—whatever they might or might not be—let them fall as they may. Like a game of pick-up sticks.

She closes the door behind her and climbs into bed, having determined that the fitted sheet is stretched tight and smooth—any fold or bump will banish sleep. She clamps her eyes shut, summons a prick of white embedded in a ball of darkness like a stone inside a snowball in reverse. She waits for the light to throb and grow larger.

She can begin. She gives thanks, she is—but suddenly she isn't whatever she is or would like to be. She isn't however or however not she is feeling.

Her parents are in the hallway. Both of them talking at the same time.

Who's the little man? Who's the mucky ducky sailor boy? Oh he gives nice kisses.

Now Em hears the excited arthritic scratching of Skye's paws on the wooden floor. The thirteen-year-old border collie is likely the last of what had been the family's long string of prize-winning herders. The den's walls are papered with ribbons, the shelves weighted with trophies. But her mother's bad hip means she can no longer attend trials and Em's father claims not to have the heart to attend without her.

Em has never made sense of her parents' devoted canine love or their sadness now that so many of the pooches have passed—adored, much-beloved creatures bearing names like Promise, Beep, Darin'. Em never warmed to them. To her they were all alike—interchangeable eye-stalkers, foreign and powerful. There was seemingly nothing they couldn't overcome, except for the fact that they were dogs.

She rolls onto her side and burrows her head into the pillow. She can remember coming home from school soaking wet one rainy lunch hour when she was eleven to find her mother kneeling on the floor under the kitchen table, massaging Beep's gums to calm him—he was petrified of thunder. Em heated her own soup, took down a bowl from the cupboard. She turned off the stove and spooned from the saucepan, pausing occasionally to watch her mother knead small circles above the dog's teeth, under his nose. All the nerve endings were rooted there, she explained to Em, keeping her voice low. The idea was to relax him, coax him from his tranced quaking and panting, tail needling between his legs. Em stopped eating and shivered, feverish. Rain shot the window over the sink. This, she thought. Finally, this. She felt herself embarking, her life an avenging, onrushing raft.

Now that she's in her twenties Em finds it consoling to picture her parents growing verry verry old, their skin crepeing like elephants but their memories fissioning until they're unable to recognize each other—toothless, noisily gumming their Pablum suppers like words of love gone rotten. Em will visit them, she thinks, not often but when she can, in the nursing home. With any luck they won't know her anyway.

She imagines their confusion deepening, widening, swallowing them up. Their eyebrows arching as they search through their vast stores of gibberish for the lost syllables of sense. As if sense were a home—the houses they'd each grown up in and left forever to start their own family—intact but rolling away, the wind huffing and puffing and blowing it across prairie and moraine, hill and dale, those long-dead dogs of theirs chasing it down, their small sturdy bodies flaring flat open like flying squirrels.

Em is certain that in the end all her parents will remember will be those dogs.

She turns again onto her back. Sleepily she lifts her cami. Her rippling abs, well-displayed in warm-weather running garb of shorts and bra top, console her.

Like counting sheep, she fingers her ribcage, enumerates guy lines and under girders. Everything in order. A tender hurt pools left of the mole above her right nipple. Desolation and pride. Ever the spanners into the works, she can still hear her parents in the living room now, cooing at simple Skye, or is it Bart? When it's not as if he could peel them a grape or get away with murder.

We don't need you.

Two days after Em's last visit with the couple, she now immediately recognizes the reception she's getting from Marta—Em has been trained to identify and manage confrontational, blaming behaviour. Indeed, the woman's anger and hostility are right on time, righty-o. Necessary stages on the path to her acceptance of the great event about to befall her husband.

A loose jiggling sensation spooks the top of Em's head. A migraine coming on. Trying to ignore it, she studies the gerberas—three orange and one unearthly-looking, chalky pink gathered in a blue vase on the nightstand beside Ken's bed. Lying face down next to the vase is a card and a sprig of glowing cherry red ribbon. All the colours, all colours, suddenly gain in intensity, vibrate. Em re-crosses her legs, quiets her hands in her lap, tells herself that soon she will say the right thing. It is her gift. Her right, alrighty. She is chosen.

It's just not working out, Marta says, sounding as if she's addressing a servant, courteous yet firm. Leave us, please.

It shocks Em. She has just been dismissed.

Affronted, she waits a beat in hopes Marta spontaneously manifests a hairy chin, a squint. That she transforms into a toad.

Please, Em then mimics—and lets her eyes graze across Ken's prone, suffering flesh. The man himself has already almost completely withdrawn, cocooned with his own final inner preparations. Em takes her time, feeling restful. When she is done she lobs a glance at Marta and registers the open incredulity. A hovering second and Marta's expression settles on hatred most psycho. Ghoul, she says thickly.

Em feels dizzy. Behind her now-shut lids colour pinwheels, silver ethers pullulate. Her migraine recedes, her cheeks sting. She unshutters her eyes and regards Marta with keen satisfaction. You hurt me, she whines silently to herself. Satisfaction morphs to raw relief. Marta's done it—Em can hate her back and feel justified. It's like unwrapping a long-awaited, much longed-for present. Birthday girl.

She steps on a dead rat's nose, shrinks away. Notices the testicles, wishes she hadn't. What kind of person notices rat testicles? Worse, why should she care that she does?

She steels herself and gingerly nudges the rodent to the side of the track. She resumes her 6:15-mile pace. Interval training at her old high school—a five-minute drive from the local marina, so it makes sense for the occasional vermin to show.

On the way to the track she'd driven through quiet residential streets, lawns and rock gardens amply, artfully lanterned and sentinelled by statuesque oaks and maples, cars presumably secreted away inside garages and carports since the start of the dinner hour. Inside the houses, lights were on, TVs. Rolling by she had an echoey fretful sense there was something contained within these walls she was supposed to know but didn't.

She rests, sipping her energy drink. Recalling those coiffed homes, she has a distinct feeling of unreality. In a corner of her brain skirl endlessly receding planes, rotating views labeled one through pi barely captive in water-blotched blueprints. She must be dehydrated, her body's electrolyte imbalance and depleted glycogen stores playing tricks with her mind. She swigs heartily from her bottle, hopes she won't have another headache.

She undertakes another mile. Part way through she notices a knot-like sensation where her heel conjoins her leg—tendonitis. A marked decrease in flexibility, as if she's growing a hoof.

She feels badly in other ways. Her earlier exultation at having duked with Marta has faded. What if she lodges a formal complaint against Em? The last thing she needs is to go down tainted in her files as a narcissistic freak with affect-deficit issues. Making it unscathed through div school and getting one's own parish is difficult enough these days, what with everyone and their auntie getting religion—something about the job market, the economy, the hellishly fragile world. A rill of abjection scorches along the skin on her back like a lacey ruff, a spongy mushroom-like sensation, a lamella burn. She is tired so she speeds up, a trick she learned from coach Doug down in the big city, where she trains during the school year.

After a lap, she checks her watch on the fly. Shit, shit. She's working harder only to go more slowly. She can tell that her form is off kilter, strides uneven and inaccurate, shoulders jutting far forward in front of her hips like some weird animal concoction. A jackalope with citrine eyes and an amethyst for a heart, unnaturally animate, its locomotion strained and awkward as it transports itself. It—she, she wryly muses, stopping, hands on her hips—would stink something awful. An annihilating, dreadful funk that would protect her from extinction.

She doubles over from the waist. Halved, she stretches, panting, lets her tongue unravel from her mouth and hang loosely over her salty lips.

All through July, on her ten-, fifteen-, twenty-milers, the dying fringe her vision like wheat-coloured plumes of grass waving at the sides of roads. Wish-wish. God-speed. She can't believe she might have jeopardized her position, such deliciousness, by messing with that Marta person. Em has kept away like crazy, as much as she can and still keep her position.

One evening she stands on the shore of the great cold lake, a light wind shirring her hair as she cups the small weight in her hand. She has driven here straight from her workout. It is almost dark, should be, but the sky is bright with clouds lit with a lingering damp. Rain likely lickety-split.

She side-arms the small rock.

My man. Colin, or was it Case? Her most recent death. Way to go, Case.

In school they call it a release ritual, a little something to help the helper find so-called closure. The stone drops into the water and sinks instantly—this is the corpus. Her own personal belief is that the psyche remains consumed within her, a mossy stone turning, polishing her inner walkways—those refined allées foot-printed with her legion of dead soldiers who live on, a part of what she has experienced. Closure indeed.

She takes off her shoes and socks and wades in. Within seconds her feet, ankles, calves, knees are aflame with cold, as if shod in giant furry mukluks of fire. Then they're numb, vanished.

The horizon too. The shoreline, its cicatrice of grain elevators and bridges. And further in, the dream-like contagion of buildings. All is fog, levitation. A minefield of sand and gravel and eternal sleep.

Colin, Case. And Ken, though he's not dead yet. Hanging in there against all odds, she reminds herself.

She feels crafty, sly. Then she feels restored, renewed, blithe in her belief that things will work out for the best. Ken's Marta likely won't complain and if she does no big deal, Em can weather the resulting storm. She is that strong. Back at her car, socks and shoes on the roof as she unlocks the drivers'-side door, she stands alone, unvanquished.

Refutation—a tattered flutter, ragged movement in the corner of her eye. A better look yields the shape of a man sitting atop a picnic bench, hands in his pockets.

What is belief? Hope, with its sunny unblemished contours, shadowless valleys. She wishes for fishes—that instead of legs he has the single scaly appendage of a merman. That he's her own clever fantasy replete with gills. That he has a great smile and means her no harm.

She smiles at him. This is faith.

He doesn't return the favour.

She snatches her footwear and crabs quickly into the car and secures the door. She reaches beneath the seat and snags the hidden canister of pepper spray and hooks it onto her lap. She peers out the side window. Better safe than sorry.

The man swings his beanpole self erect and sways forward. His face is raised and he appears to sniff the mildew breeze. A haze veils his eyes. The forehead protrudes. The skin over his face is waxen and for a second, as he closes in on the car, the flesh melts from his lips, baring pitted black stumps. He is carrying something. Before she can start the engine and get the gear into drive, his arm scythes and a rock, or a tin can or marble, hits the windshield.

She is several blocks away—a heart beat, a wink—before she notices the shatter pattern, as if once-invisible joinings embedded within the pane of glass have jarred loose. She sucks at the roof of her dry mouth. Pray? She'd hate to overreact.

Ken dies quietly, Marta's fingers interlaced with his, the nurses tell Em. As if she would care. As far as she's concerned, her parents have also ceased to exist. When she makes an effort to really take them in during these last few weeks of her residency, she sees flour and fat bound with water, like those giant tasteless cookies people buy at malls, nothing but caloric content. Nothing she'd really want or couldn't live without. Or it's as if Em has blinked and, like that, her family and those she must administer to—with their ponderous, mopey complications—are gone. She can't imagine any of them anymore.

At last she drives away south to the big city, to her final year at school. Heartland, wasteland, she thinks as the hours string along. She can barely contain her speed to a sober fifteen-twenty over the limit. Her teeth chatter. The landscape grows increasingly insubstantial. Thought-curds clump in her head.

She rolls down her window, filtering, sifting the air for once-familiar impressions—dirt, gasoline. Nothing registers. Anxious, she rolls the window back up. Paste-on towns, an earth puckered with life-forms—calcareous crops, livestock too numerous and varied to tally, dragon-flies and locusts pressing themselves in mad blurts to her car windshield, everything else flat planes, a husked place. How might she attach herself? Her own voice in her head is whispery and faint.

She takes her eyes from the road and a truck blares. With a juddering effort she keeps between the highway's painted lines. She feels she is traveling great distances, gaining inch-es. She stops for fuel at a large interchange and is surprised to realize she's been in the car for hours. She is so stiff she can hardly scuttle from pump to bathroom where she pees forcefully, brutishly, like a goat.

Back on the expressway, she fingers two freshly aris-en bumps on either side of her head. She prods and pokes, claws, mauls. Breaks off to glance at her nails and sees blood.

She has been getting somewhere, she is pleased with her progress. She's put some real miles on her feet in preparation for the mid-October marathon, which is two weeks away. Seven more days to go before she can kick back and taper to easy short runs, carbo-load till the cows come home.

At five-fifty a.m. she meets up with her running group by the waterfront path, nods hello all around and unzips her wind jacket. She silently gives thanks for being in school once again, for having acquitted her clinical practicum not much the worse for wear. Over by coach Doug she spies the guy she's most recently interested in, downing an energy gel—a peacock of a plastic surgeon, likes to run with his shirt off even though the first frost is nearly here. Impossible not to notice his six pack and tell her those aren't pec implants. Put a shirt on! she wants to scream at him. Date me! she wants to roar. She has always had a thing for attractive, eligible members of the Hippocratic profession. So when, after the three-mile warm-up loop, he cuts out from the pack and heads along a thin defile of underutilized track, she pursues, though she loses him instantly in the pointillist pre-dawn.

But she's no quitter. Light welts through the in-between-season trees of the park. This morning, this great lake a damp gray bandage. Tenebrous tree tops pitchfork, striating fascia-like into the echelons of infinity—another shatter pattern, rip in the illusory fabric of wholeness. To which she pays no mind, distracted by a stitch in her sinistral side, vanished before she reaches the underpass, revenant by the time she attains the harbor.

She is tired so she speeds up.

Among the pealing sparrows, the doxological crows cry praise in their midnight robes—virus vectors, disease amplifiers sparked with razoring intelligence—and bursts of iridescent starlings true to their namesake bust like tiny stellar jewels across the heavens. The inhabitants of the soft-loft conversions awaken and the great city marshals its inexhaustible resources that ripen, in time, for her specialized services. As she bruits the footpath beneath buttresses of hickory, sycamore—vast plantings in carefully planned tracts—not for the first time does she marvel at the foresight, the tremendous vision of it all. Until not ten feet in front of her a man who is not her doctor-man steps out of the hedges, blunt object in hand. If only she could just power by.

A schematics of rock, water. A dormant humming, sub-vocalize of earth and ants and worm castings, bat guano's springy bower. Mufflers of mauve-tinted cloud. The early growing traffic a bee buzz through contracting pipes of sound. Her canopic skull in figments she can't hold.

Me, she manages to think as her limbic regions stroke out for good. Em.

As she is, faceless among the hostas.

Armada

The first Jesus from my father's mouth, the Rabbi startled, then he rolled—*Baruch* this, *Adonai* that, what a pro. Soon my father looked like he was boiling, curses bubbling into the December air. Twice I tried to take him by the arm, get him to settle, maybe coax him along the shoveled path and put him in the car and lock the door on him. But no go. Each time I plucked the sleeve of his old duffel jacket he shook free, swore like a stevedore, some of which tribe he'd once known personally—before retirement many years ago, he'd been the general manager of a shipping company, contending with layoffs, strikes, Ukrainian stowaways, the city in those days still a major port.

Jesus all through Kaddish. All through my brother, soft in youth but now stiff as a sword in his black overcoat, occasionally flicking a drop or two from his face. Beside him his stick thin AnnaMaria, shivering in her tiny wrap, un-gloriously underdressed for a Hanukah burial—Jesus, hard to believe. Apparently her only dress coat was red. Apparently not even she had the nerve to pull that off.

At least the freaking cold was working in my favour, since beneath my parka was a pantsuit that used to fit but was now tighter than drying rope. Earlier that morning, dressing in my mother's disorderly bathroom, dizzied by thoughts of what to keep, what to toss—useless for the final journey her dull manicure scissors, eye cream, four nearly finished jars of Vaseline, what the fuck?—I'd handled my belly fat then sucked it in and yanked the zipper, tortured in private places.

I was thinking though that the cold could be even colder. I imagined a rent-lung clarity, vapour, a vacuum-packed nothing. Freedom through freeze drying. Rebirth as astronaut-drift in an unblinking beyond. Escape.

Instead there was the snow. Was it ever coming down, fogging the surrounding hills. Leaving not much to look at except each other, the hole in the ground, and the lilac-coloured coffin, dainty, impractical, pre-selected by mom herself and about to be wholly surrendered while we blinked, unfathoming. We were fudged, smuzzy. Something we weren't before.

For one thing, we were in a section of the cemetery reserved for the deceased of a local Labour Zionist congregation. My father, who hadn't attended a service since my brother's bar mitzvah, and certainly counted himself as no member of any group, had purchased the double plot here because it was by far the cheapest available, in his books a moral victory of sorts. Making small talk with the Rabbi pre-service, my father had make-believed about synagogue so-and-sos there was no way he knew, holy days he'd last celebrated in the Antediluvian Era. When the Rabbi asked how many years my father and mother had been married, the answer was a fantasy beast of a fifty, the best creation had ever bestowed.

A creature called Dummy, I'd immediately thought—what my father used to call my mother when, during their frequent fights, he broke a lot of furniture trying to break her warrior silence. Hearing my father's lies, I'd wanted to call him out. Of all times, I'd fumed, re-tightening my thick scarf. Of all places.

But with the Rabbi reciting and my brother mumbling along, my father totally lost it. Jesus, he shouted, tears streaming his cheeks. Jesus! I steadied my gaze on the shovels spiked like spears in the hard dirt heaped around the grave's perimeter. There was scaffolding too, and wide straps, some kind of gizmo for lowering the box and conducting the business at hand.

I kept my back turned on pretty much everything else. I'd already seen there weren't many mourners hanging around for any of this. Only AnnaMaria managing, despite her shaking and quaking, to leaf her hands through her thick hair. Only a few unimportant relatives—an aunt and uncle, childless people my mother had never cared much for. No friends.

My mother had been embarrassed to have lung cancer. Years of smoking, what she'd openly referred to as her filthy habit, had caught up to her. When she'd received her diagnosis eight months ago, I'd worked to convince her not to say she had breast cancer instead—which she thought might gain her greater sympathy, pink ribbons, stuffed toys, balloons. Some prize. The whole thing made me realize how much my mother must have lived confused in her head. My own head swam just thinking.

So when my father began racing the wooden plank alongside the grave, backing and forthing over the now-descending casket with its cargo of emaciated sheet-wrapped body, I let him be.

The purity of that sheet had been important, evidently. Keeping it that way had caused some consternation.

I'd driven all night and part of the early morning to arrive at my parents' apartment crammed with a riot of meds and a ripe cat-litter box, my father exhausted and possibly incorrectly, dangerously drugged into brief acquiescence accepting coffee, a buttered roll—the bread not too far past its use-by date. And—the phone call. This from some clown at the funeral home. There was a problem. In accordance with custom, they'd wrapped my mother—what was left of her—in a white sheet, but as sometimes happened with the dead, the guy explained, she was a cauldron inside of stomach acids and bile emitting a staining fluid at the mouth.

Took me a moment to comprehend. The only way to keep the sheet pure was to sew her lips shut. Permission was being sought. My father, too out of it to deal, passed on the matter.

I didn't hesitate.

All those times I'd begged. Eat, please. Anything, especially toward the end. Mushy pasta with bottled over-salted sauce. Simulac by the teaspoonful. In those last months I'd desperately tried to ark as many calories as I could into her. Get her to pack some on. Get her to live.

She hadn't wanted any of it.

Yes, I told the funeral guy. Yeah. Go right ahead. You do what you need to do. Do it!

He seemed taken aback, stammering a few words before cutting short the call.

I hadn't cared. Here was some news. All along my mother had been full. On her surface, mute suffering, blankety-blank. Inside, a delicacy of churning eels and lobster claws click-clacking—*tref*, impure, an unbridled unclean. In death she was well provisioned. The proof—just some foam breach-burping the surface.

But here now was my teetering, imprecating father, here was the snow curling like the crests of waves over the leagues of the dead. While I was taking my magic carpet ride into the past. Please, the Rabbi was saying. I'm afraid. Your father could fall.

My brother started and the Rabbi shrugged apologetically and peered at his shoes. Hefty numbers, scuffed and salt-soured, clearly they'd seen better days. Like his face, the flesh listing, skin pouchy and pocked. He was not an attractive man. Tell AnnaMaria that though. Unmoored from my brother's side, she hove closer to the Rabbi and was cocking her hip, maneuvering her trembling bits and pieces. Now the Rabbi looked really scared. Worse, instead of directly retrieving my father, my brother dallied, selecting the best shovel for the job to soon come. This lawyer in his fine cashmere blend, former brat who from the ages of four to twelve my best friend and I picked on mercilessly, before he transformed into an untouchable teenaged Doobie Central, all torn jean jackets and Lynyrd Skynyrd black armbands—I had to admit, watching him now as he hefted the shovel, he'd manned up nicely over the years.

Jesus, Jesus, my father called.

The Rabbi shot me a pleading look. Like I was the one prolonging things indefinitely.

I walked. I'd done it before, a lot. The second I'd turned eighteen. Cities, provinces, countries, whole emotional territories shipped and skipped. Good riddance. So I walked forth to collect my father and possibly dodge my brother, thinking big deal. Soon I'd return from whence I'd newly arrived, to my bullshit job tallying columns of numbers for a questionable nonprofit and my squamous low-rent apartment squirming with learned bullshit papers—though I certainly couldn't be said to have sailed through school, I had over the years amassed degrees this, degrees that until I was an impoverished pack rat of esoteric knowledge, with murderers and thieves for neighbours. Someone with places to go, people to see. Including a new young guy—the young dudes getting younger while I got on—who I was secretly entertaining designs for, and even more covertly not.

I went. This time toward what was left of my family. The wooden board nearly bestride the grave was soaked and slippery and I inched toward my father minus my mother—my father chuffing and capering bareheaded since, moments before, a flapping gust had disappeared his yarmulke. At the opposite end of the pitching plank, my possibly pre-pre-divorce and probably very fed-up brother was walking too.

Took a death grip to halt my father's wind-milling right arm. Just in time, as my brother now bore straight toward us with his shovel. Jesus—who and what were we anyway? Uncivilized, bereft of dignity, sure. Otherwise, I had no idea.

Not that I was beyond imagining some other life. Desire like melt, river runs throating deep-cut banks. A cock-salty, scorched caramel scent to the stirring breeze. Not that everything had to be about sex, but.

I was so there.

Until I remembered. On my way here, gripping my device with one hand while steering with the other—scudding between ruts and potholes, mind trammeling apparitions of black ice—I'd called my oldest best friend from the road. This after speaking with my brother, father, weeping, scratching and gouging, packing, canceling meetings at the office.

My cell was for once getting brilliant reception.

Becca, she rasped into the phone—before she'd found what she called her spiritual center as a born-again, she'd been a shit disturber of epic proportions. Becca, she graveled a second time in her semi-destroyed voice. I'm so, so sorry.

And then, before I could so much as get a sniffle in sideways, she went off on her sister, Kitty. There was a John involved. Or a Shawn, or Sean. Cast of thousands.

But Jen, I managed to get in, choking back a plug of snot. How's Doug?

Surprised me, for sure. Doug was her recent ex-ex who, for a not-so-recent while, had been mine. Why ask about him now? I swear sometimes, my brain!

Doug? Jen said, then paused long enough for me to think the connection was a wash.

I stayed on. I thought I could detect a sinking, rising sound, an aqueous sub throb, a forked-tail flick. I wished.

Then Jennifer's voice, shark-skinned and unlovely, resurfaced. She said, Doug is Doug.

I got off fast as seemed polite under the circumstances.

I'd been surprised to still be there, in the car, north-easting I-94 and so on, so forth—December, the billboards of once-fantabulous Michigan. Eat Here, Eat This.

What there was of my family rocked, our rent-a-Rabbi rolled. Father, brother—who were they and what was I to them? Around us, the tall pines waved their arms hello, goodbye—maybe in their language these were the same word. If I squinted, instead of wet snow I saw apple blossoms. I opened my mouth. I closed it. I didn't want to think what might be in those flecks, the dreck of dead, cold-kissed stars. I didn't want to think. And yet hold on, I thought, unsure of what I meant while amid the bare trees, across the snow-swept swales, the winter sparrows dervished like dreidels. Like there was so much to cease to know.

Made Right Here

After the rain Bryce lost Serena in the cave. Not the cave with the original horses falling and giant aurochs. And the stick-figure guys with evil-looking spikes boning their chests and limbs? Sign of the vision quester, according to the English-speaking guide.

Though this concrete-and-rebar bogus fronted all that. Fake and fakes to protect the goods from humans with their trash oils and gases. Humans, right? Walking body bags.

Not that Bryce thought of Serena in those terms. He shouldered through the tour group on the raised wooden platform, searching for her—pale skin, wide blue eyes, cropped black hair nearly shaved on the sides. Her solid build and height not a match for his but still, should it be so hard for him to at least glimpse her?

No luck. Damp and uncomfortable, he shoved toward the path's lip and halted for a second to get his bearings, leaning over the railing above a cubby where the halogens didn't reach. The plasterer's wall seam didn't escape his notice and neither did the screwdriver jammed in among the fake rubble on the floor. He scrambled again to retake his rightful position next to his wife so he could once more point out the cheese of it all. His wife, whose idea it was to come here to begin with. To see the ancient paintings. For inspiration.

Instead, randoms. Everywhere he looked.

The old feeling returned. Bryce choking on hooks while some douche superior pounded his back and congratulated him for nailing another probable dipshit. His old days in tactical—unholstering at every reasonably credible fuck you and you too. By his second year of marriage, third on the force, Serena screaming at him, I don't want you fucking dead, you fucking idiot, I swear I'll divorce you. By then they both knew he'd never finish his night-class degree, never make detective, just like his old cop dad never did.

Serena's threats convinced Bryce. Take the seven-thousand pay cut and months of ball-bruising training to secure the rank of captain in a mounted squad. Take crowd control at Springsteen concerts, tourist duty in Grant Park.

Better than the lineups of most-likelies and close-enoughs strung together as if on his dad's old fishing line and drawn through Bryce's intestines, barbing his throat even now in this sorry-excuse not-quite cave in France. The south of France. In this fake cave beside the real cave. Drove him crazy. He couldn't understand. Why bother?

Because better Serena.

Hey, what's the hurry?

Watch yourself, okay?

A tight trio of girls in front, Bryce nearly wheeled to deal with the bright remarks from behind. But even with the artificial lighting, the dark tunneled humidly above him and his brain sirened toward Serena, well ahead of him like always.

The Buffys shuffled on. Gulping clay breaths and something sharp like tin, Bryce edged closer, waiting for an opening in their ranks. The yammering continued in his wake. Where does he think he's going, anyway? Who does he think he is?

These guys. Bryce had them made outside, ticket stubs jutting from hands, halt-go descending the paved ramp with the rest of the tour group in a drizzle soft as the strands of a web. The gray-beard Aussie sporting hiking pants with a zipper around the knees, a matching khaki shirt and one of those joke safari-style hats with a chin strap. The short, gym-built German in fancy sneaks sizing Serena up near the food cart, so help him. Their asinine questions. How much longer? Any chance you have extra brochures? Borrow your map? Askholes.

Like Bryce once upon a time. Asking away, asking for it—whatever *it* came his way. Hey, what're you doing? through winding alleys while punks' pit bulls monstered for his blood. One time not long before he put in for his transfer, some asshat unchained a snarler who gave not a flying for the vest. Until thank-god Luis, Bryce's partner, who Bryce never even liked that much and still doesn't, drew and dropped it. And wasn't that a lot to think on? Still a lot?

Watch himself? Seriously? He hunched his shoulders and lowered his head in the dank not-cave air. He almost turned.

But the girl-knot in front of him loosened and he scraped through. Some luck to remind him of the lesson he apparently still needed to learn. At least he was safe for now. No thanks to himself, he had to admit.

Take that, German dude, Bryce thought, then added a mental pat on the back for himself. Couldn't resist.

Forward lurch. For something like forever Bryce single-filed, feeling huge and useless, sandwiched like meat between civilians. It killed him. The walls heaved closer with every step, he swore. The ceiling shrank and he crouched as he went, the skin beneath his jeans clammy, his torso furred with sweat beneath his shirt.

The walls curved leftward and the semi-dark grew semi-darker. He spanned his arms and scooched his hands over the slippery cladding. When he took his hands away, his fingers felt sticky and sore as if stung. His eyelids half-shut as if swollen. The air smelled foul-sweet, like cough syrup. The guide's miked voice crackled incomprehensibly through speakers mounted high on the walls, then died with a loud click. Bryce's tramping in and out of time with those around him drummed the wooden path in tricky rhythms that coaxed an ache deep in his skull. A low hum prickled his chest.

For all he knew he was getting no closer to Serena.

He forced his eyes open another crack. Spot-lit wall paintings of upside-down purple oxen crowded red-outlined horses with black manes and tails. They all seemed like poor sketches that someone forgot to erase.

His pulse reared in his temples. How far in was he and how much farther did he have to go? Beat a retreat or keep on?

How far along was he anyway?

His claustrophobia only increased. He wanted out. Now, as in yesterday.

Breathe, Bryce told himself. Breathe, fucker. What else could he do? Throw himself on the ground and hyperventilate like a suck until a stretcher arrived. Or meditate the way his therapist and Serena told him. In with the good. Out with the bad. Flush what felt like sleeping bats from his lungs. Or was it in with the bad, out with the good?

It killed him to not remember.

He managed to hustle, no harm done, past the elegant older couple he'd previously noted, brown skinned and well dressed. So there was that, Bryce thought.

And now this large white lady. No kidding, he had no time for large ladies. Ma'am? *Madame? S'il vous plaît?*

Finally she turned. In the fudged light, the face on her. A brick. A painted brick with an exaggerated slash of black-red lips and pencil-lined brows. A fright-wig frizz of dyed blond that stuck from her head in a joke halo. The lips began to crawl and Bryce nearly jumped out of his skin. *Monsieur. Allez, allez. Tout de suite.*

But she refused to budge. She was saying other things too but he could only figure so much, and that much thanks to Serena's tutoring, thanks to her art college French elective from nine years past, ancient history. Bryce could scream. *Madame?* And when Her Largeness smiled a mean crooked and waved her fat paws, cruelly shitting him as she held her ground? He wanted to roar.

His fists clenched and his throat scorched. He blamed France. The French. Did they even ventilate this hole?

With a soundless gasp he sucked his gut to his spine and pressed past the giant-lady cans.

He could puke but no stopping now. Nearly home free. Home—meaning Serena—or bust. The whole point, right?

He was crapped out at last into a great domed bubble he guessed at fifty feet floor to ceiling and well more than twice that in length. He halted, awed despite himself.

Floodlights swept from above and below and still failed to entirely illuminate the chamber, the vastness like something from Bryce's childhood yearnings—a spaceship in empty space, somehow suspended in the middle of his bedroom at night while downstairs in the living room Dad and his moods screwed with Mom, or vice versa, and shit went sideways.

For Bryce, in bed upstairs, this mega floating. No Mom and Dad. No bedroom window or fall breeze rustling the sycamore's leaves as it brushed the window panes. No cold spring soccer games behind school after school. No school. Zero scarred-knee Tom or scab-elbowed Josh bombing bikes to the Lucky Superette or late-summer long-afternoon shadowmen on lawns, heat fevers. Zip snow days or Dad's lake trout singing in the frying pan. No slug of tongue trapped in Bryce's mouth and dying its wet slug death night after night, rain or shine. No crying. And each night, if he concentrated enough, nada even on what he wanted so badly to see that he nearly saw it. No Bryce even. Just a rising into a dark so dark no stars infiltrated.

The rest of the tour group straggled in and dispersed. He stepped to one side and waited for his eyesight to adjust to the spooky lighting.

For the first time since entering the replica cave, he felt decent. Since entering France with its cheese after stinking cheese, to which he was beginning to take hard offense. Serena's doing. Her *while in France*. Which she'd only repeated seven times a day the past week. He guessed each one counted for each year since she'd graduated and mooned over the idea of this trip. And so the cheese stench off him when he relieved himself each vacation morning, because even in France she kept him to his celiac's diet. Which given their budget, as determined by Serena, permitted a lot of the stuff on the affordable picnics in the according-to-her storied parks of Paris. The meals, the locations—she'd masterminded it all.

His gut gurgled. He again sought a sense of the room's largeness. Beyond the floodlights, scallops and crests in the stucco ceiling resembled a brisk breeze stirring water, frisks of fish there for the scooping—what he imagined as a kid when his off-duty dad disappeared dawn to dusk, though Bryce begged to go too.

Now, on the cave floor, his fine feeling completely vanished. English and French and whatever sloshing whateverly around him, Bryce thought he might as well be seven again, waking alone to a rabid babble in the middle of the night. Dying for the aliens to rescue him.

He scanned the perimeters of the cement ballroom for an exit. No escape as far as he could tell.

Besides, Serena had said *here*, so here he was more or less. It was another question where she was. He rose onto his toes and pivoted. Still no go. An obstacle course of cement squiggles rose from the floor and messed with his sightline. Stalagmites? Stalactites? Serena would know. He suspected she knew everything.

Her doing his stink and her doing his diagnosis, which took her a couple of years unearthing third-opinion doctors, deciphering insurance forms, nag-calling the insurance company. He had her to blame, he liked to joke, for the loss of his stomach ills and general crappiness. His blood pressure dropped. He dropped the meds and the mood pills. His pre- pre-diabetic blood sugar resolved. This past week he half joked that he blamed her for his good fortune.

He knew it wasn't entirely fair but right now he blamed her for this fake cave.

For a second, studying the strange formations before him, Bryce thought he heard her laugh. He trotted to the ballroom's far side.

Then he was unaccountably muddling among the outcroppings. Swirls laced the cement in peculiar patterns. One twisty formation, thinner than the rest, extended floor to ceiling like a flimsy support, as if it alone kept the cement from crashing down. Condensation dripped with little urgency around its delicate curves. If Bryce wanted he could snap the thing in two.

He thumbed a groove and thought again how Serena planned it all. The trip. Today's tour. She'd scrimped more than usual given his pay reduction so that with the new improved Bryce she could freely ogle the tapestries and sculptures and other foreign whatnots she'd once studied in school and even now copied in weird ways into what she called her work. Which he could never for the life of him figure. Not the copying. Not her paintings. But his confusion didn't matter. Not to her. She'd cut costs and strategized and today driven the tiny rental car south. During the drive she lectured him on how these reproduction cave paintings and this cave had been constructed over the course of twelve years to mimic the authentic one next door, closed to tourists.

She'd frowned when he scoffed. Went as deep silent on him as the indecipherable reveal-conceal of her art.

Like the spaceship of Bryce's childhood, the meaning of her enterprise fatally eluded him.

A businessman and businesswoman. Matching gray suits, black briefcases, identical scary-scarecrow smiles. Flattened looking, like road kill. Surrounding them, a border of olden-time ladies in long purple dresses lounging on carpets of grass while white unicorns nuzzle the women's laps. Kid hefting a baseball mitt and grinning his whole body at a blue sky. Instead of a ball in his glove, a stone inscribed with Egyptian-looking hieroglyphs. Beneath his feet, boulders incised with same.

Serena herself—a reasonable copy thereof—with her black spiky hair and high cheekbones and black-rimmed eyes. She's sitting naked on the toilet in their very bathroom. Very naked. Stretching her arms over her head like she's sleepy, nipples erect. The mole on her left breast sprouting its three wiry hairs, which she refused to pluck. Three replicas—only much longer—waving from her business-as-usual bulging outie like giant insect antennae. Worse, a weird smile on her face, same as in the other paintings.

So many paintings, from a foot square to six by five or more. Sometimes Bryce caught himself imagining there were some too small for him to notice. And some so big only a god-eye could make out the pattern, fit everything together into a whole that made sense. Either way, things she'd been at without him knowing, her way of keeping him in the dark.

Her paintings played tricks on his mind and on hers too. When it came to fixing Bryce, she was all over it but her own so-called work dragged her down. She'd spend long days in her basement studio, then peg each new painting unframed over the couch in the living room. In Bryce's off hours he'd watch TV and catch sight of her in the hall side-eyeing her handiwork. The looks on her always mashed his heart. Hope. Fear. Distaste. Distrust. More hope. After a moment she'd vanish around the corner. Hey, what're you doing? he sometimes called but she never answered, just creaked up the stairs and shut the bathroom door. After a while he'd hear the toilet flush and the water run. A few days of this and he'd come home from a shift and the painting would be gone. Probably added to the stacks downstairs and in the garage. Occasionally over the years he'd nose around and notice the stacks had disappeared and new ones sprouted. He learned better than to ask.

Sometimes she scrutinized Bryce the same way she did her paintings, the exact series of expressions messing her face. On the drive over to her friend Janel's for dinner or in a crowded movie theater, robots and rockets rattling the screen, he'd catch Serena at it. What? he'd say, and she'd shrug. And then for a few days something like Bryce would hang on the wall above the couch. Recently on his mount Scottie, who Bryce hadn't warmed to yet. And was considering replacing, seeing if it were possible, getting a replacement. In the painting, poor dumb Scottie, only better. Regal, not the drab creature retired from competition hunter events by his former Ritchie-Rich coke-head owner and donated to the force. Rumour was she'd turned her life around through her love of horses—of Scottie—then forgot all about him when she went off to some swank school. Bryce imagined her married eventually to a rich broker who'd knock her up with two kids of her own and stow her in a four-bedroom, five-bath in Wheaton. The kind of place and people Bryce and Serena scoffed at in the old days as boring and spoiled. Unlike Bryce and Serena. A cop and an artist. As a couple, how original was that?

The old days, he thought now. When did they end, anyway?

He still believed it though. On his own he didn't amount to half as much as he did with her. She added value, for certain.

Though they confused him, her paintings proved it. In the most recent one, both he and his horse sported lips flayed wide by guywires and pulleys into smiles so broad it pained Bryce to contemplate. A giant lance tucked under his left arm jutted protectively beyond the animal's arched neck while a small sword stuck through Bryce's poor celiac paunch, which spilled pink roses. On each—visible when Bryce peered super close at the canvas—stitches of scoffing inchworms.

An earlier painting featured Bryce on bended knee in a yard of tall dark blue flowers, beaming while rat-sized bees scurried through the air. Nose to paint in the living room, Bryce noted the tiny gold-bullet buttons on his brush-stroked dress blues, which for real he mostly only wore for the funerals of his brotherly-sisterly fallen.

Original, all right. He got what he asked for. Mostly he was okay with it. Sometimes though he wondered what Serena saw when she looked at the real him. Him? Or some other Bryce she'd fashion to her purposes.

Sometimes Bryce, the real Bryce, wanted to shake her.

Calling all spaceships, Bryce would then think, recalling how as a kid the thought had soothed him.

It helped now too, in the cave ballroom, as he remembered the times when she was in the kitchen and he'd knelt on the couch and examined the paintings and felt sad and a little dicked with, perusing the tiny studs of white funeral-type flowers reflected in his spacey ice-cube eyes. At each inside corner, a single melt-tear.

Another loud laugh. It came from the front near where the rat-faced guide likely lurked, confirming another of Bryce's suspicions.

He veered over the lumpy fake ground, gulping crap air.

Tall, sturdy, in truth it was her—the flesh and bone he stretched alongside night after night, bunked cold. Made it. Bryce wanted to scoop her in his arms and give her a twirl, cheesy as that might seem, before making the hell off with her.

Too cheesy. Plus she was faced away from him, otherwise absorbed. He could hear her snickering at something the guide had just said.

Bryce hip-checked her. Not hard but she startled. In the uneven light she seemed paler than ever.

Hey you, he said.

She glared at him for a second. Not even. Hey yourself, she chuffed, already again turning her back.

Before he could get out of the way her small fancy knapsack knocked his chest. She'd bought the bag on sale, after what seemed to him like hours of deliberation, in a Paris department store, calculating the exchange on her phone's app, slipping the straps over her shoulders and mugging in profile for the mirror while he lurked behind, squinting at herself, uncertain if she liked what she saw.

Wounded, Bryce retraced his steps and wandered anew among the cement formations. They were soft gray, jagged in places and smooth in others. He studied their swirls and grooves as if he knew what he was looking at. For whose benefit? he wondered, feeling dumb as dirt.

After a moment the outgrowths seemed oddly familiar. His hand went to an itch on his brow. That was it, he realized. In Serena's paintings, tiny knobs with curious markings—some bizarre symbology—grew from his forehead, just visible beneath his riding helmet, his dress hat. Strange he'd forgotten. He knelt and inspected one of the formations at length, top to bottom and, craning his neck, from all sides. With its ridges and lines, it bore a resemblance to carved bone. Like his painted baby horns, except all grown up.

He wondered what to make of that.

He got to his feet and brushed off his pants. He touched his sweat-oiled face. As usual, aside from the faint impressions of dimples, it felt as unremarkable as putty. Of the two of them, and despite her protests to the contrary, Serena was the striking looker.

He listened for her again. Chitchat burped around him. Nothing he could identify as his wife.

He felt his temples now, massaged his entire head. His goddamned heart seemed asleep in his rib cage.

One night, a seven-year-old Bryce realized that the vessel of his deepest desires, which he'd never seen but had taken to imagine hovering a foot above his bedroom floor, possibly pre-existed him. Maybe it had been waiting patiently for eons, for some slow-rolling irregularity in Bryce's retina or a slipshod iris to burst awake and reveal another world. Or rashes of them, like the constellations of blisters on his legs when he'd waded into the poison oak behind his aunt's house in Janesville when he was five. Because who knew how things connected? If they did at all. And if they did, what could he do about it? Bryce lay nearly paralyzed in his bed, his parents at it downstairs. His thoughts spun. He forwent his nightly tracing and retracing of the faint shapes of cowboys on his jammies, not knowing if he felt less or more afraid to reach for the glass of water on his bedside table, to get up to pee and forget to flush. His brain felt both very large and very small.

What couldn't he do?

He hadn't known then. He didn't know now. Though for an uncanny second he almost felt the cave might have something to tell him. As if alive, it wheezed—he could feel puffs of air pushed by the creaky ventilation system, tickling the hair on his forearms like a tiny wasp might, an intelligence universes distant from his.

He froze.

And then he shook off the thought as Scottie might a fly. Shit together, Bryce ordered himself. Get real.

He tagged Serena, flocking among the Aussie dickwad, German dickwad, big-dick lady, girl dicks. Bryce found it hard to decide on the other couple, nearly old, identically handsome, quiet except to murmur between themselves and never seeming to leave each other's side, but he ended up deciding anyway—dicks. His head hurt more as the guide led the way beneath arches and through a cave room of illuminated display cases. They contained bone tools and wood-handled brushes with dried grasses for bristles. Hollowed stones used as candle holders, the candles with wicks of juniper, the guide said, which would have burned a white smoke that didn't damage the artwork. More passages followed this room. Purple aurochs—big-ass horns on those oxen, Bryce noted with satisfaction—and deer and horses fanned three or four deep that would have flickered into movement in the candlelight, according to historians, according to the guide. Some of the creatures upside down and some sideways, as if from the viewpoint of a spinning beholder, maybe one of the stick-figure humans who appeared quilled through the chest and limbs—every now and then the guide parked and barked these theories, arms woozing back and forth as if he hoped to conjure the original haze. Through it all Serena cleaved to him, her spiky head bobbing.

If he wanted, Bryce could theorize about that.

Good for Serena, he thought. How nice for her notebooks and sketch pads. Her vision boards—her words for them—that she tacked to the long western wall of their basement. For what? She'd never sold her work. The last time she exhibited at a gallery, a single painting among a dozen by other hopefuls, she'd priced herself to extinction. In Bryce's view, not that he'd said. Six thousand for a canvas too large for most people to hang in their place? That was several years ago. Nowadays she attended the major dog shows, setting up a table and easel and drawing people's prized Poms and slobbery Berners—from photos, not even the actual dogs. Cash only. She actually bragged once that she knew every ATM location in the convention center. Bryce had just grunted.

According to Mr. Expert, this cave, so-called, featured more than six hundred animals. How many pet drawings had Serena done? So good luck to her with all that. How nice for her if she found the inspiration to keep on with her work. If inspiration was what she needed.

Bryce rubbed the nape of his neck. Salt prickled his vision and he imagined smoke thickening the passages, his thoughts sharpening instead of dulling.

Serena was a cop wife. She might hate it but there it was.

The walls closed around him again. He tried to stretch, reclaim some space—but people. He accidentally brushed the German's side. The German actually apologized.

No prob, Bryce said, pressing his finger to one nostril to siphon air in through the other, a trick his therapist showed him. He felt his chest reopen.

The problem was, he admitted now that he could think more clearly again, his mom had been a cop wife. She drank alone until his dad took early retirement after testifying against some buds. At least in those days they let you go, no questions asked. You came home permanently to fish from shore and drink with the rest of the retireds who had lacked the smarts to hustle enough on the side to buy a boat. You trolled and tippled with the near-indigents who not only caught but ate the sore-studded carp, you shot the shit with off-duty hose draggers not even casting much but probably just trying to clear their sinuses of the black char of babies lost to house fires in Englewood because their parents were too drunk or drugged to properly ash out. Anyway. Once Bryce's dad retired, he fished and drank and in his absence Mom drank. And then Dad came home and drank and the two continued to battle.

Serena though—she was a cop wife, but more. She drank but not much. Bryce didn't touch it period. Not since his first and short-lived attempt at shedding the fam when, in his early twenties, he booted it to Toronto and camped at a waitress girlfriend's for a year. Bryce an illegal, not working. Boozing like the old guy and gal and freeloading off his own gal's shrimpy earnings. Not proud of that. But he was proud that he hadn't seen his parents since he and Serena married. Good on he and Serena, right? Beating the odds, fingers crossed.

He continued to spy her now in the cave. The planes of her face angled to the arches and shadows. Her shoulder shrugs. The fast tilts of her head to her left side when she was pondering. So her.

Still her, Bryce noted, with relief. Hair crisped to sharp points despite the earlier precip, she looked like when he first met her in the bar on Damen she tended when he was new on the force and new to moonlighting as a bouncer. Serena. Great name, he'd thought when the manager first introduced them. Great ass but also no-nonsense with her slashed jeans and waist-looped chains and paint-spattered Docs. He'd liked her straight away. Really liked her. She seemed fearless. Puke in the toilet? She mopped no comment. After a knife fight on the floor—Bryce up the street grabbing a gyro, re-entering approximately ten minutes after it happened to a lot of blood and the club mostly cleared—nothing from her except her usual gruff last call and lightning-fast cash-out. He suffered calling that one in but had to admire the backbone. Morning classes, earning her BFA, the dishwasher told Bryce when he asked around. Her Art Institute attitude returning his initial interest with a few snotty once-overs and then ignoring him for a month. Not much got to her in those days, not even him.

And then suddenly, it seemed in memory, they were shacked together in his apartment off Irving Park with a kitten called Stoli—poor Stoli, dead of cat AIDS before the age of two. Until then Bryce had never known such a thing existed, just like how until he met Serena he'd never seen such undying love for Henry Rollins and weirdo Russian art from hundreds of years ago featuring thin sorry saints. Or Bryce's own stunned love for her when she set up a workbench in his living room with paint tins and brushes and knives and sketchbooks on the floor. Twice daily she pasted first his and then her toothbrush, an act he learned to return in kind sometimes and when he washed the pots and pans after dinner—when they did eat dinner together, depending on what shift he worked—she'd grip his waist with her strong hands and dry hump him from behind and whinny like a fiend.

She stunned him. They married. He took extra shifts and she graduated and quit the bar so she could paint full time. She was alone a lot. Over time—which Bryce imagined now in flickering layers like the cave horses—things did get to her. He got to her. She got to him. He told her to stop texting him so much when he was at work. She got a budgie, Marcel the purple budgie—Bryce noticed that much, didn't he? He cared. So what did Marcel do but fold up his little wings one day and die. Serena tucked him in a small gift box with tissue paper and headed out the apartment door that night carrying a large metal serving spoon. She returned minus the box and spoon and with mud on her boots. Bryce noticed all that too. Did she for a second think he didn't?

He'd listened to her crying over the years, her pleas each time a cop fell. Thanks to her he joined mounted, rode around like a grinning ape for a fraction of his former pay. But he did manage to float under the radar of the latest cop inquisition, though he was pretty sure Luis might have to squeak soon, that or jail. And Bryce couldn't thank Serena, he knew, for the thankless fact that someone seriously tried to kill him—with a dog, of all things, and Luis had to go and have Bryce's fucking hind-side. To be saved is to owe. So that was pressure too. He didn't need her crying to remind him.

Worse, recently Serena declared she wanted a dog. A big dog. For company, she claimed. For security.

He couldn't seem to explain the deal to her. For fuck's sake, he had a horse. Think about it. Okay? Enough with the animals. He had. A fucking. Horse. His job. Get it? His extra shifts. Unless she could start making a bundle with her animal portraits, charge way more than thirty cash per at her dog shows, cat shows, monkey shows for all Bryce knew. If she could do that, he'd quit. She could get herself a dog then, get it?

She got it. Did she ever, she told him. She got all of it all right, every day of every year they'd been together and one day sooner or later she'd have enough of getting it. His killjoy fear poisoned everything she did, everything she tried to make, coloured how she saw things. What about him? Didn't he ever get anything? Couldn't he try? For once. To get it. Would it kill him?

Here in the cave, the old words boomed in Bryce's brain. *His* fear?

He couldn't keep track. The fuck was there to get? Remind him. He loved her. Didn't she still love him?

He saw the problem. A cop wife like his mom, Serena was lonely. He tried to picture her solo at home on the couch, waiting for him, worrying. Getting off her sleek butt and out the door to jitter past the taquerias and dollar stores of their Chicago hood.

But what he imagined best was Serena here in the cave by herself, getting fired up, no help from some guide. Not alone, but with Bryce himself by her side. A Bryce who knew for once what to do.

The group herded into a new passageway. The guide droned on. Bryce managed to sidle up to Serena again. He reached for her hand. Got it. It felt cool and rough and his mind went white.

He put his mouth to her temple. I'm glad we're here, he whispered.

She reared her head and squinted at him.

Bryce felt his face flush. He hoped that in the dark she wouldn't notice. No, I mean it, he said, too loudly, sweating cheese, helplessly aware of his suddenly cheery booming voice. I do, he went on. I really do. Thanks for dragging my arse these thousands of miles.

She tugged at the straps on her knapsack, then looked away and coughed. Her breath stank like something dead. The guide frowned in their direction. She slicked her lips shut.

Only once did Serena take him to meet her mother.

Judith of Blue Island, Serena called her. Our Judith of the School of Hard Knocks.

But Judith was okay, he'd thought, permitting him during that visit—a year into Bryce and Serena's being a couple—to light smoke after smoke for her in the cramped kitchen of her Blue Island bungalow over refills of diet ginger ale, no ice. Hurts the chompers, she told him, tapping a crooked incisor then tightening the belt on her flowered robe, though it was past four in the afternoon. He got it, agreed, hurts. He'd had to pull all the strings his rookie brain could to score a Sunday off—the only day Judith received, because Penney's six a week was hard work and only on the seventh was she rested enough to greet some rookie hump. But he dealt, because Serena. And so for a couple of hours he and Judith smoked and drank their sodas and griped about the weather, a winter Sunday just a few months before he and Serena would marry at city hall, already dark outside with filthy sleet. Judith asked him to fix the leaky washer in her sink, which he did. He changed the burnt bulb in her oven and offered to return in a few weeks to clear her gutters of dead leaves.

At which Serena—on her feet the whole visit, stomping between the tiny kitchen and living room and bathroom—hustled on her leather jacket. She bumped his arm on her way to the back door and flung it open. Last call, she snarled.

In his bewilderment, Serena's over-bold lipstick—she'd gone full makeup like a mask for the visit—permitted him to register the words as not really hers. He hunkered in his chair, head hanging, waiting for what else.

Judith, though, rose like a queen. Head high, spine erect, her robe billowing in the freezing draft, she laughed bitterly and offered him her hand to shake. Look after Rebecca, would you, Judith rasped. Not a question but a command.

Rebecca? Befuddled, bemused, Bryce stumbled to his feet and laughed as colour flooded his wife-to-be's face.

Then he felt guilty. He turned on Judith, laid on the indignation—Hey, I'm not stealing her, is that what you think?—and she unwrapped a sad smile.

Serena recovered fast. Mom, she sneered.

It sounded like an accusation. Severe of Serena, Bryce thought, shrugging on his pea coat. At least she had a mom. A mom wanting or at least willing to pretend. One not shut up with her booze in a dark closet of a living room.

But Serena was all about the straight no-bull mode. Which is what Bryce had bought into. So when he never did see Judith again—her no-show at city hall the last straw,

Serena declared—he let it drop. He figured Serena's silence on the subject let him off the hook of future family complications. He'd guessed that Judith was still kicking, since there'd never been a funeral to attend. And as for Serena's dad, he'd been even less of one than Bryce's. She claimed to have never met the guy. So Bryce shrugged that off too, figured better no dad than bad dad goading bad mom.

With Serena ahead of him again now in the cave, Bryce leaned against a wall and faced the way he'd just come, wondering what good his looking back was doing him, or Serena. The remaining stragglers clomped by. The German passed, venting a small *ha* that struck Bryce like a pat on the noggin. Ha, yourself, Bryce muttered after the guy, who turned briefly, the smirk on him grown smirkier.

Bryce told himself he'd be outside soon. He'd fill his lungs. The drizzle would have cleared. The day would look like another better day. He'd throw an arm around Serena's broad straight shoulders and she'd grow limp against him. Hungry? he'd ask, as if that might help restore her.

He was sure hungry. Thirsty too. It was as if the place had drained all the liquid from him, wrung him dry despite the dampness. Soon dust would be all that was left of him. Not even an outline.

Bryce?

He wheeled. Serena stood on the narrow wooden platform, showing a lot of teeth. She shook a clear plastic bottle at him and the water rattled.

Thanks, he said, leveling his chin and trying to match her smile. I'm good.

She unscrewed the cap and swished. Then she drank, throat squeezing. When she was done, she swirled the remaining inch of liquid. You don't want some? she said.

For her sake he tried but his parched throat wouldn't close and some water dribbled down his chin. He handed the bottle back to her and she polished it.

Where we going tonight, again? he asked. Some other castle you've dug up?

She slowly screwed the cap back on.

Oh-*kay*, she said.

It is okay, he said quickly. No problems here. We're good.

She snorted, drew herself taller. No, we're not, she said and swiped clumsily at her mouth with her hand.

L'eau. Low. Bryce pronounced it silently a few times, as he'd done last night in the fancy-pants castle restaurant, getting up the nerve to ask the waiter for a refill while Serena slurped her—surprise, surprise—third glass of wine.

Maybe she was right. They weren't good.

He chewed the inside of his bottom lip now and faced her down.

She glared back, face a dull gleam in the dim cave. Want to know something? she finally said.

He waited. He shifted his weight. At some point you'll let me know? he said.

All we've ever done is get old.

This Bryce could deal with. You're not old, he said quickly. No way. Never.

You're not listening, she said.

Last night, cicadas had clamoured just beyond the window near their dinner table and farther off, in some thick shrubbery—a hunched shape darker than the growing dark—a bird insisted. *Bon soir*, a woman near the bird suddenly chirped. *Ciao*, a husky voice, male or female, answered. *Bon soir*, Bryce had repeated in his head. *Ciao.* Made up for the silence to which he and Serena treated each other over their stringy quail, and mushy pears for dessert. He'd headed to their room by himself while Serena took some air, as she put it. He'd scowled at himself in the bathroom mirror and pasted his own toothbrush. Air, for fuck's sake. He thought of doing her toothbrush but left it naked and got into bed. He never heard her return, though she was next to him, lightly snoring when as usual he woke panicked at three a.m.

In the cave she crossed her arms over her chest. Her fingers twitched like spider legs. Except for getting old, it's like we've never changed, she said.

Nothing wrong with that, he said, encouraged by her use of the plural.

Same old idiots, she hissed, leaning toward him, face a contorted mask.

Her venom shook him. He pressed his knees together, as if he were sensing Scottie ready to spook at an extra-rowdy crowd. Ride it out, Bryce ordered himself now. Yee fucking haw.

Not catching your drift, he offered and sucked in his cheeks to flash some dimple. That used to defuse her every time, a long time ago.

Her eyes glittered. Bryce's gut needled and for an instant he saw himself wrinkled and unshaven, in a small gray room in the center of a jumble of hallways.

Come again? he said, dogging on anyway.

I'm always less me. You're just more you.

Come on, Serena, he pleaded. I don't get what you mean.

She uncoiled fast and snapped her fingers under his nose. *Voilà*, she said. Right you are. You don't get it. You never will.

Merde, he muttered occasionally, practicing. At one point, choked for breath, he stopped and placed a hand over his chest. *Merde*, he said, as if swearing a solemn oath.

If she didn't love her life or him in it, he would let tactical take him once more. Whatever happened between he and Serena, this was his decision. She could leave him for rejoining or stay with him and hope he died. She was a cop wife but more. Or maybe she would decide she wasn't.

Serena? Bryce said out loud now in the cave, though no one was there. Hey you?

He couldn't tell her in this fake cave anyway, Serena awed like in some church. He'd tell her on the plane. During the dinner service, the second movie, whenever. She'd rise from her center seat and crawl past him on the aisle. He'd clink the ice in his first scotch, why not? Sip from his third somewhere over the unseeable North Atlantic in a grey clarity his, all his. And then fuck it, down the hatch, while she took a long while in the bathroom.

He wished they were on the plane now and that he'd already told her. Seat backs and tray tables in their upright positions over Chicago at dawn, its light-grid warrens he'd sight as the aircraft swooped lower, ready to land. Or in their terminal at O'Hare already, Serena streaking ahead of him toward baggage claim, soon swallowed by the crowds.

Now he thought of her as she'd been in the first few days in Paris, this wife he nearly couldn't recognize. He paced onward toward—he hoped—the fake-cave's exit, picturing the Serena he'd thought he'd known. Almost there, he told himself. Nearly home free.

The lights flickered, snapped off.

He halted. Knees shaking, he waited for his vision to adjust. But he must still be too far inside the cave. No external light penetrated.

No up or down, left or right. The floor twisted to the ceiling. His head whirled and he dropped a knee.

Serena's paintings came to him, fuddled with the cave's falling red horses. He rode tall on Scottie and Scottie, near obsolete in real life, fell, toppling Bryce. The images shifted and raced in place, paced by occasional blanks—silvered cloud banks portending cosmic rain, soaring blue that signaled all clear, Scottie full gallop. Flip flip. Bryce wielding a lance or charger—whatever those knights of old carried—that vibrated above Scottie's arched neck confoundingly like a giant diving board over ocean.

Astonished, Bryce dipped deeper into his vision. Scottie's nostrils like saucers and his gait like flight—Scottie, only better. Not the Scottie in his South Shore stall waiting for Bryce to return them both to duty at some boring Irish parade or outdoor Nirvana tribute band concert. Scottie not knowing it was all over. Asleep on his feet.

All We Did

Any man with a ponytail, any man twice our age—this was our thinking way back when, what passed for thinking. Any man changing the marquee after hours as we rode the streetcar past the second-run movie palace. One of us swaggered off at the next stop, dirty slush up to her ankles but so what, her baby-fat body not yet a bulb she'd blown, winter white not yet her favourite colour.

In the aisle of the theater, rows of faded red velvet seats, rank and file, observing like cattle. Forget-me-nots in the carpet.

Spring came. She tried all things. Which when we think about it now, how quaint.

Pregnant once and never again. Cramped for weeks after.

She went away. She came back. Everyone who'd stayed looked the same, terrific, inexhaustible. She left again, and when she returned everyone had vanished. She was in need but the buildings were mute. Mother dead.

Father too. The sister she never had. *Cinema Lumière* an expensive isolation.

Slowly the flowers release themselves from our fingers.

Nostalgia one tough slog. Along the avenue the trees are still beautiful, naked with snow so pale they're like girls' boys, premature. With perfect recall she is falling down drunk and laughing on every corner. A moving van mesmers by, its crew anxious as suitors while on the sober cul-de-sacs, behind closed doors, a euphony of TVs make mockingbird song.

For all that, she manages to inhabit herself enough to play well with others, get and hold a job.

At the Ministry, the jingle-jangle of intergovernmental meetings fits her public-complex ambivert excesses so swell. It's official—she is a definably valuable human resource, there is a memo that says. The way she likes her coffee, the endless upgrading of skills, the steady paycheck, the backaches, stomachaches, benefits—she is the usual dichotomous self of the acute-stage, sleep-deficit employee. Her private enterprise thrives like a hothouse weed. Stuffed away in her cubicle she is her own dream board, she has if not friends then allies, she networks like crazy. Madam Prime Mover. Wee Willie Dinkum. Among the addendums everlasting, she has her peace plan.

It *is* working. Is so.

Still she dreams of clean breaks, a start date that says Now instead of this confusion with Then. She begins to dream her old apartments, dreams she loses the baby in a pile of old newspapers, a mausoleum of distracted words. Hopeful. Hopeless.

The returns policy. Must have the receipt somewhere. The one that says, If Opened, Item Cannot Be Returned. Some way of determining Best Before, or Best After.

Meanwhile her apnea episodes spike and spike and spike. And each time she wakes, she wakes extinct, tongue draped over her airway, uvula collapsed, the once-stately architecture of her slumber a ruined ghetto, remnants carted off, tourist trinkets hawked cheap in the grottos of penny remorse.

Nothing a long hot shower, a good dubious look in the mirror won't cure. One, two, buckle her shoe. A tonic sick-day hike past bungalows, parkettes, the shallow heaven slung with wire conducting information loads, low-grade illuminations. She is *Only the Lonely*. There will always be *Last Tango in Paris*. Another *Deception*. A sky shorn of cover opens its deep blue Wi-Fi throat until, in the splendid manufacture of her hypnagogic hallucinations, light hisses off the metal-glide surfaces. Office towers, car windows, a woman's unfettered lip gloss. Shush. There, there. Such solemn deflations. What's left is what only the wind gathers. A bouquet of swings swinging in a playground.

At the office the next day and the next she continues to be continued, neither here nor there. Weeks pile on like tinder. Hang-fire months. Eventually somebody notices and it goes straight to the top. There is *The Conversation*. Lunchroom plots abound, subplots, repetitions. She gets her well-deserved time off—no really, the Ministry insists.

Problem is, boredom afflicts like flies. Her leisure hours a fistful of loose change, like words of pity instead of coins pressed into the leathered palms of the homeless. Words like Forever,

Forever. Each one subtly distinctive, though they boomerang back, knock her flat on her moribund keister. From the chaise under the smoke bush in the yard, days a certain violet shape, gravid. Nothing leaps or cries out to be saved. There is only the innocent spite of the hydrangeas, the way with callous indifference their frivolous heads ornament the empty morning.

Pins of sunlight needle down.

At bedtime her continuous air pressure machine—her better half—keeps her going, her airway forced open. For this she wears a mask. Boo. Let loose upon the world, all she does is turn in, early.

Still we do what we can, we keep the faith, and every spring irises return, dwarf reticulate among the vestigial snow. We keep it coming, remember her in summer, a white dress shawled with rain, a celluloid flicker. Amaranth, belladonna. We dream a place she left, forever notwithstanding.

She dreams we little fuckers ignite.

She has her own ways of being true.

Her wraparound shades won't save her, nor the love she ever made or waged. What she sees, we see blind. Peas in a pod, everything we look at looks the same. Our love like our fury binds and abides.

Maybe if we did the math. Acknowledged the strapping teenaged daughter. Husband. Mother-in-law. Snug as bugs in some enchanted-in-the-usual-way abode not far from where she and we were once one together. Throw in nice neighbours. Just try. Fatloads of good. Stones in a stony field. What any of them do all day we have no idea. We know no one who knows her. We refuse to. We simply, simply refuse:

The Association

Where are you? Martin's mother says when he calls. She sounds groggy, not her usual self.

Martin is in Virginia Beach with his dad. Or not quite with his dad, who is here to check out—Martin's dad's words—a certain bass player at one of the bars near the boardwalk, while Martin keeps his own counsel in the motel room. *His own counsel* is a new phrase of Martin's, gleaned from one of his TV shows. Martin is eleven. His dad is in a band. After a thirteen-hour drive, he and his dad arrived straight from Chicago around dinner time and now it is well past. Martin is supposed to be in Rehoboth with his dad. His dad is supposed to take him for crab cakes and fries and hot pie with caramel sauce. He is supposed to buy Martin a boogie-board, though it's June and the water will be cold. In the morning his dad is supposed to take him the short drive from Rehoboth to Gran's in Perth Amboy.

In the weeks before his dad picked him up at five a.m. this morning, Martin and his mother agreed he would only call in case of emergency. He peers at the low stuccoed ceiling of the motel room and swipes the sweaty hair from his eyes. He crinkles the plastic bag lying next to him on the mattress cover. The labouring air conditioner barely flutters the closed curtain. The window looks out, Martin knows, onto the parking lot. The motel is near the highway and not within walking distance of the beach. None of this, Martin knows, is an emergency.

Put your father on, Martin's mother says when he doesn't respond. She sounds more alert now.

Martin pops a hard candy in his mouth. Sour cherry. He clicks his teeth against it. Next he will try the banana taffy his dad bought at the last service plaza at which they stopped.

Where is your father? Martin's mother says. Martin?

I have to go the bathroom, he tells her.

Don't hang up, she says, enunciating with the cool precision she might use with one of her patients. Put your phone down on the desk, she says. I'll be waiting for you.

There's no desk, Martin says.

All right, she says evenly. On the nightstand. Is there a nightstand?

Martin, she says in her clear, unflappable voice when he returns and picks up again.

Yo, he grunts.

I'm here, she says after a few seconds.

Here, he thinks, and pictures the old apartment before remembering they've moved. He brings the taffy close to his phone, scrunching it between his ear and shoulder, and unwraps the candy so she can hear him do it. He chews loudly.

Why don't you describe the room for me, Martin? she says cheerily.

Not much to describe, he thinks. But he will leave it to her to decide what is important and what is not. There's two beds, he mumbles.

Good, she says. Thank you. Any sounds?

Martin pulls his ear away from the phone. The mini fridge buzzes. A few sad clanks for attention from the AC unit. Surf, he tells his mother, struggling to get his tongue around the sugary plug in his mouth. Big-ass waves, he lies.

Martin, his mother says, then coughs to cover her sternness at his language. See? she says, in reset mode. Pretty neat, huh? Tell me, what colour are the walls?

He has no idea—the walls are walls. He wrinkles his nose and swallows. The room smells bad, flobby, a made-up word he'll tell her if she asks. He fixes on an unevenly painted square above the TV, which is not working. There are uneven squares everywhere, he realizes, spying another above the closet, others in spots near the ceiling. Drab, he thinks, the walls are drab, though he knows that is not a colour.

He considers that yellow might please her. He recalls the Post-its tabbed on the doorframes and banisters of the new townhouse he and his mother relocated to on the South Side this past winter, the neighbourhood occasioning sneers from his aunt and uncle—his mother's older sister and younger brother, North Siders. His mother's flags bear handwritten instructions—NO NOT HERE! and FIX THIS CROOKED!—for the workmen who still arrive every week to finish what the builder should have completed before Martin and his mother took possession, as his mother refers to it. Martin thinks the townhouse will never be fixed. He mostly ignores his mother's written directives, which are not addressed to him and which, in his view, serve as poor replacements for the framed prints and family photographs that once hung in the sprawling, floor-crooked Rogers Park one-bedroom he and his mother shared with Martin's dad—mementos now stored in the townhouse garage. As such, Martin thinks—liking the sound of the phrase, sometimes used by an evil lawyer type on Martin's favourite rerun series—as such the notes are also like the mutterings of the adult world, like the continuing arguments between his divorced parents that do not concern Martin. Over his head, out of sight. Nothing he can or needs to do about them. His mother will deal. As such, the notes make him feel safe.

Martin?

He picks a jawbreaker from the bag and contemplates it. Yellow, he tells her.

She gasps happily. Yellow, she says. That's exactly what I was thinking.

He wakes cold out of the covers. There is a kerfuffle—his mother's word, he realizes despite his haziness—outside the motel-room door. He hears a woman's voice. A man's. Martin's dad, Martin realizes after a moment. The woman squeaks a few words Martin can't make out. Bullshit, his dad says, laughing. Martin drags his heavy legs under the covers and snuggles down. Bullshit. As such, the rest is blank.

Martin is the boy who eats all the candy and he knows it. He is a Lab Rat. This means he is smart, very. He can do what he wants, to a degree. On this July evening three weeks after the botched beach trip with his dad, Martin grabs a fistful of Gummi bears from the fancy bowl on the granite counter in the neighbouring unit, everyone cooing at the kitchen upgrades although they're here to attend a townhouse association meeting. Martin's bravado—another newly acquired word—causes the rest of the neighbours to glance meaningfully at each other and shake their heads. Martin's mother gives him The Look, reserved for moments like these when they are around other people, and which he disregards.

Moments later he hulks on the end seat of the white sectional in front of the French doors leading to the Juliet balcony—terms bandied by the milling adults—and ignores the bullshit. For example, the bullshit that is his mother's hopes that the neighbours whose unit this is will take a shine to Martin. They are a childless couple who both wear chunky sandals and stiff cargo shorts and pink short-sleeved shirts and hold doctorates in neurobiology. Jewish too—like Martin's mother's side, she has lately become fond of pointing out. She smiles like she has a secret each time the couple acknowledge Martin's existence, like right now, the man stumping toward Martin offering a glass of bullshit tap water and a napkin to wipe his sticky mouth, pointing to it with the napkin and making a wiping motion. As if Martin doesn't know his mouth is sticky.

Martin stares straight through the neighbour. The man looks confused. Frowning, he places the tumbler on the coffee table, on top of the napkin on top of a coaster, and retreats to a seat in a folding chair by the glass doors.

Martin knows a lot. Like all the solutions to the big-snore math problems at the Lab School—the school the reason why he and his mother live here, so she won't have to keep driving him every morning from the North Side where they used to live and she still works, and reverse drive in the late afternoon. Martin also tears through the outcomes to the biology and chemistry experiments, way faster than most of the kids whose parents are faculty at the university to which the Lab School is attached. Parents who, according to Martin's mother—who is not faculty at the university—receive a hefty discount on their children's education, unlike his mother. Parents who might win Nobels one day, according to their kids. According to Martin's mother too, who plumps with pride when Martin returns home from after-school science enrichment and tells her the scuttlebutt, as she calls the kids' brags. Just home from work, she adjusts the collar on her blouse and straightens from her usual exhausted hunch on the display-model couch she boasts she smartly bought for a song—a real couch, not like the futon-frame job they had in the apartment in which Martin had until now grown up. She tilts her chin and smiles her knowing smile and draws back her shoulders, displaying the remnants of the powerful upper torso of a former college two-hundred-yard freestyler champ.

Swimming was how she met Martin's dad. Martin knows the story, which his mother was once fond of relating. She'd finished her laps in the pool at Columbia U and, upon levering out of the water, a tall young man strutting the deck caught her eye. Failing to catch his, she re-entered the water and lapped him several times, hoping and failing again to impress as he crookedly backstroked and unashamedly treaded water. This went on for months, the same time once a week, but never on the same day of the six she trained.

In exasperation one afternoon she full-on went for it—maneuvered herself from her fast lane into his slow, passed and then waited for him at the deep-end turn, jammed her leg into his creaky pivot and met his glare with a compliment on his stroke. They married a year later. Another year and they had Martin.

Martin knows the rest of the story too, what his mother does not relate. His parents divorced after ten years, and here Martin is now, with his mother in the neighbour's townhouse. Bullshit bored.

More people assemble in the living room and Martin ignores them too. He concentrates on his modest earache, a recurrence of his childhood infections. He wonders if he can claim the clicking pressure in his head as a reason for returning to his and his mother's own unit. But she takes a seat in the large easy chair opposite him, her soft stomach mounding on her lap, her chin up. She's wearing her superior smile.

Martin nudges a dish of cashews on the coffee table toward himself while his mother clears her throat and leans forward. Her wire-rimmed glasses are smudged. Visible below her baggy white shorts, her legs crack with purple veins. Her frazzled, grey-streaked mane frays around the shoulders of her oversized T-shirt. She clears her throat again and everyone continues to ignore her.

I believe we have a problem on our hands, she says into the swirling chat. The problem is the easement. We're leaving ourselves wide open.

Martin scores a haul of nuts and sits back. Might as well, he thinks.

The easement? the woman neurobiologist says sharply, interrupting the various conversations, and her husband snorts into his hand, then gazes at his woolly toes.

Martin's mother squints craftily. I propose, she says, that each unit chip in, so we can hire one smart cookie of a lawyer. And see about jointly buying out the easement rights.

A few outright chortles from those assembled. Martin grinds a paste between his molars. Since his parents' separation, his mother has become an expert in lawyers. She frequently speaks of suing people—for example, the townhouse builder—and obtaining multiple legal opinions on subjects ranging from her contract at work, which leaves her underpaid and unhappy, to her living will, which she wants to redo for the third time since she and Martin's father split. Martin thinks if his mother could sue his father over Martin's latest earache she would, if only she could prove the infection was caused by his father's negligence. Had he or had he not insisted on making Martin shower immediately following his sole and unwilling dunk in the ocean? He had not. But Martin has decided on a personal policy of shrugging away any of his mother's lines of questioning concerning his dad. Things seem simpler that way.

Please, another neighbour groans. A lawyer?

I know one or two, Martin's mother says, face lit. But we should interview five or six, and make each sign a confidentiality agreement. You never know.

The neighbours seem to avoid each other's eyes, unsure of where to direct their attention. Helpfully, Martin lets his lower jaw drop open and his coated tongue protrude. He ignores the startled expressions.

His mother is looking at him but not with The Look. This is one he's never before seen. He ignores it too.

Hours after the townhouse meeting, by the gleam of his computer screen, Martin dislodges cracker crumbs from his keyboard. He tugs at the scratchy bandages his mother has wrapped over his ears and wriggles his pointer finger beneath them to poke the wadded cotton balls. He runs another algorithm then closes some of his programs for the night and turns off his screen. He stands and for a disorienting second the still-unfamiliar carpeting swells and falls. Dizzy, he considers calling for his mother, until his eyesight adjusts and he makes out the reassuring hallway light at the bottom of his bedroom door. His mother's clear voice suddenly carries from her bedroom. To whom am I speaking? On her phone again. The floor settles beneath Martin's feet and he mounts his bed, still a novelty to him. In the apartment he'd slept stretched and dreamless on a mattress on the floor of his room while his parents crashed together on the futon sofa in the living room—life when Martin's dad was still around, in those years when Martin's mother was finishing med school and then hardly sleeping at all through her internships.

Like the parents of his classmates, Martin's mother does important work too. At the VA on the North Side she is a psychiatrist who medicates criminals, as she refers to her patients. She mostly knows them by their social security numbers, not their names. Some of these people, she confides to Martin, are more criminal than others. Some of her work is Top Secret, for the government, and some of her work means the late-night phone conversations. Does Martin understand?

she sometimes asks. What Martin understands—aside from Homeland Security maybe and maybe global peace—but neglects to let on is that she will never win a Nobel, like some of his classmates' parents, as the award would require everyone to know what his mother does. As such, Martin can't brag about her Top Secretness. He can only keep it secret too, storing it in his chest where he thinks of it swelling his soft stomach and floating his man-boy tits, inner keeps where he hides other secrets too, other tales he refuses to tattle, no matter the temptation. Like the one about the boogie board his dad promised and then neglected to buy Martin to make up for his missed dinner a few weeks back. Or the mere single day at Gran's—because his dad just had to book, as he called it—instead of the three Martin was supposed to have. And she was upset and had words—Gran's word—with her son—Martin's dad—and as such forgot to make the Oreo cheesecake Martin likes so much. And the trip back to Chicago taking three long days, Martin's dad stopping at crappy towns to hear bands and leaving Martin alone in the dinky motel rooms. At least he'd finally kept himself from calling his mother, watching, instead, a lot of bullshit TV.

His dad. What a fuck. For fuck's sake.

Martin arches his eyebrows and makes a mock O with his lips. He clamps his hand over them. Language, he thinks in the voice of his mother.

Martin is also not supposed to yank off the bandage itching his right ear. He wads the material under his pillow anyway and by the dim light inspects the outlines of posters on his walls. Electro, Gakutensoku—the pictures of vintage robots are among the only decorations from the old apartment his mother has allowed in the new place. Their outdated programming and vaguely human likenesses fascinate Martin. They're the past imagining the future. The future's past.

Sometimes Martin's mother tells him he's not doing his best to cope with their current situation—their referring to Martin and his mother and not his father anymore. His father, Martin understands, is now fully in the past, the future's past. But his dad is a far less good deal than the robots.

Martin's ears hiss and sputter. The sounds remind him of the surf on the late afternoon his dad finally shook off his hangover and shuttled Martin to the beach. While Martin's dad strolled the boardwalk, Martin kicked at sand flies for twenty-six minutes, according to his phone, before his dad showed up coffee in hand and ordered Martin—minus the boogie board he'd been holding out for—into the water. For fuck's sake, Martin's dad grouched, a quick dunk won't kill you. Neither will taking two minutes to get out of that big head of yours.

Later, while his dad chatted up some girls not much older than Martin, he shivered on the boardwalk, damp towel around his shoulders like a bedraggled cape, shaggy hair uncombed and filthy, he was sure, with microscopic bacteria. When the girls left, his dad insisted on buying Martin a fortune printed on a small yellow ticket stub from a mechanical fortune teller embarrassingly named Zoltar, a crap automata wearing a turban and silk vest—Martin's school pals Shehan and Jyoti would have flamed it with sarcasm, not to mention the fortune itself. You will love wisely or not at all. Lucky numbers 17, 201, 6. What bullshit, Martin's dad said, laughing.

Martin had refused to even begin rearranging his face into a bullshit cute-kid grin. For fuck's sake, he thought, splashing the words around in his big head while his dad bought him a dripping soft serve and hustled Martin into the car, no shower or change of clothes, or late real breakfast or real lunch. His dad then crawled them through rush-hour Virginia, DC, Maryland, and sped like a fiend through Delaware, cursing the tolls since he had no transponder, and on into New Jersey, stopping three times the whole trip to hit the can—as his dad, somehow looking at once sunburned-pink and puke-pale—referred to it. The can. Martin referred to nothing until two in the morning when Gran tripped down her driveway lit by her buggy landscape lights and nearly crushed him in her arms as if he were still a bullshit kid. For fuck's sake, he told her, and the shocked look on her face struck through his chest the same way it felt the day his mother announced she and Martin's dad were splitting.

But no, Martin will never divulge to his mother the extent of his father's lapses. Aside from complicating Martin's day-to-day with his mom, at some point the deadbeat bullshit might prove useful in ways Martin hasn't yet entertained. As such, he is storing the idiocies like important data, something some superbad AI might one day unleash. As such, Martin believes in keeping a lid on tight, as his mother sometimes complains of him when he refuses to answer the questions she asks. Are you happy? Can you tell me how you're feeling? Describe the room? For fuck's sake.

Martin lifts his big head—the one his dad thinks he should get out of, the one with the lid on tight—and punches his pillow into shape. He will go to MIT when he's older, where he will construct bots who wreak fuckery. He knows from information his mother has scrounged that it's in the bag—the Lab Rats have a high rate of acceptance at MIT, at anywhere they want to go.

Martin locks his hands behind his neck and sighs at the ceiling, with its poster of Michael Phelps before he got busted and entered rehab and staged a comeback. The poster is an oldie but goodie, as Martin's mother says of it, the swimmer's nearly inhuman wingspan spread wide over blue water.

Martin blows a wish-kiss Michael Phelps's superbad-angel way, even though it isn't necessary. As much as he knows anything, Martin knows his future.

Unless the cancer gets him.

Because she is smart too, his mother figured out he harbours the cancer gene. She likes to tell the story of how, when he was a baby, she had him tested not once, not twice, but five times. She was that sure. And sure enough, the last test revealed his pre-diagnosis. This is why she microwaves organic pot stickers for his dinner and serves him organic apple juice. After dinner she microwaves organic popcorn and lets him fill up while he watches his shows about evil turds and smart-girl secret agents perfect as the AI Martin himself might create some day. He bets those bots won't dream at night either.

Sometimes Martin's mother will say, Anything interesting happen last night? She's concerned he never remembers his dreams—never has, as far as he knows.

Two nights, Martin hears his mother say now from her bedroom. As if he can't hear. Ten mil Zyprexa. Restraints.

Martin adjusts his bedcovers. Now his ears squeak and rustle and he feels a phantom motion, the in-and-out tugging of waves—nausea from the antibiotics his mother has him on. He considers phoning her to say, I'm here, even though she is just down the hall. He imagines her questions, so he gives up on the idea of calling. He tries to remember his old room but his mind thickens. He removes the bandage from his other ear and presses the fabric to his nose. The wad smells metallic, comforting. He hears his mother open her bedroom door and the hallway light switches off and then she closes her door again.

His thoughts lift when he thinks of tomorrow. He will run the simultaneous localization and mapping robotic programs he downloaded tonight—SLAM, data in, reaction out. Such programs can create maps using scanning lasers and then, interfacing with a bot, use the maps to navigate in real time with other path-planning and obstacle-avoidance algorithms. It's the stuff of driverless cars, robot vacuum cleaners, maybe excellent biological adventures in the future, like nanobots in the bloodstream. Like the miniaturized submarine and crew from the golden-oldie *Fantastic Voyage* Martin and his mother streamed ages ago one Friday night in the old apartment while they waited for his dad to come home from a show at a bar and he never did. Probably such programs have military applications too. Like bomb defusers and who knows. SLAM, problem solved.

Now Martin imagines his mother in bed, falling asleep with her smudged glasses on. He tucks his head under the covers. Describe the room, he orders himself in a corny robot voice. Martin recalls his posters in immaculate detail.

Problem solved, he reports. Then he laughs inside so his mother can't hear the mock-fiendish crescendo that echoes in imagined 3D over stormy seas and interplanetary space travel stations. Like something in a movie he might watch if he could convince his mother to take him to see it. He can almost get a load of the poster for it as he drifts toward sleep.

Shit, he thinks. He shakes himself alert enough to reach into his nightstand desk drawer. He tapes new bandages over his ears so his mother won't be upset when she checks on him in the morning before she leaves for work, when he is still asleep and dreamless as machines.

Martin's ears feel better in the morning but his head hurts. He's hot but the AC is turned low to save money. He tipsies down the stairs to the second floor before the workmen arrive. They never speak to him, barely nod his direction. This suits Martin fine. He drinks a glass of organic chocolate milk standing over the sink. His mother has already left.

Martin has his own work to do. He wobbles past his mother's latest Post-its to the first floor and cracks open the first-floor bathroom door. Dank air drifts out and the two cats leap from the tub to greet him. They are large, beautiful, golden with black spots. Bengals. A birthday present just before summer break from Martin's mother, with the understanding, as she referred to it, that they stay in the bathroom and Martin tend to them. This past winter, right before Martin and his mother moved, he'd seen an article on the breed in a magazine while waiting to see the dentist. The creatures made him think of Cheetah the military bot. Martin campaigned hard and accepted his mother's terms.

As such, he now fulfills his part of the bargain every day, nudging the vanity under the sink open and scooping cat food while the animals purr and rub against his bare legs. He refills their water dish and replaces it in the tub. With a plastic shovel he digs through the litter in a plastic box on the floor next to the toilet and bags the waste for the trash. From a hook on the back of the door he takes the toy, a long stick with a feathered mass on one end, and dangles it while the cats jump and pounce.

August arrives. Martin's ear infection clears and his mother drives him each morning to science camp in Evanston where he applies his mad skills. Evenings, he quality times it with his shows and sometimes fails to get out of accompanying his mother to more association meetings. At least the adult talk eddies undemandingly around him while he basks in the potent AC and perfects his scowl between mouthfuls of snack foods. He is here, he understands, to keep his mother company among the hitched. As if he and his mother also form a couple, a childless one like the Jewish neurobiologists, to somewhat balance out the two South Korean pathogen-research couples who each have a daughter much younger than Martin and both of whom are also Lab Rats. There is also a white not-Jewish couple, internists both, with a large doughy baby.

Martin does find himself warming to the idea of the Jewish couple. Oddballs, his mother has recently taken to calling them, to account for their increasing standoffishness. But of interest to Martin is the large, loud black dog they have recently acquired, an excitable pedigreed beast—a near-child only better, by Martin's count—that the man and woman parade to the nearby park. Martin would love to play fetch with the animal. By his count his own pets don't rate as full playmates or as kids, since by his mother's decree the animals exist only in the first-floor bathroom. But the couple haven't offered and Martin's mother can't get behind the idea, as she puts it. Too unpleasant that a child should need to beg, she says. I'm not begging, Martin keeps insisting to her steely smile. And I'm not a child.

There is another member of the townhouse group, who Martin sometimes forgets about. The man never attends the meetings and has refused to join the association, period, so Martin's mother dislikes him. He's a divorced financial guy, middle-aged like Martin's mother and also white. His young, pretty Japanese ex and their daughter sometimes live with him in his lot-and-a-half western end unit. So he counts as half of a couple with half a kid.

Martin's mother also dislikes the man for the money he has spent hiring an interior designer for his unit. She dislikes him for the expensive—and she means ex-pen-sive—landscaping featuring costly mature trees and heirloom perennials he has put in his yard. The man is likely on the spectrum, Martin's mother declares at the association meetings. You bet he's all about fee simple, Martin's mother likes to say in her precise, clipped voice to the other townhouse owners.

The man's teenage daughter, pretty and older than Martin—Mallory or Ashley or Allie—does not attend the Lab School. Pretty and too dumb, Martin decides, when she and her glossy friends ignore him one sweltering evening as he strolls past her dad's shady trees and shrubs, attracted by the girls' silvery laughter, their smiles flashing like minnows through the twilit-green leaves.

Martin's dad calls one night in the middle of August. They haven't spoken since the beach trip, the longest they've gone without contact. Martin is online and too busy to answer. His dad leaves a message—Hiya kiddo!—sounding drunk and also, for once, like he's trying too hard. Kiddo yourself, you fuck! Martin mouths when he finishes listening. He laughs his villainous laugh. He determines he is too busy to ever return his father's call.

Another night, after organic pot stickers and carrot sticks with honey mustard dip on the TV-dinner tray tables in front of the couch, his mother folds her arms over her chest and asks if Martin would like a dog. Summer shadows wash outside the open French doors. Soon it will be dark and Martin's mother will close the doors and shut the curtains. The room will shrink. Martin, his mother says again, eyes narrowed behind her glasses. I asked you a question.

Martin thinks. Zipping around the park with his own dog barking and nipping at his heels—until the obedience training, which Martin is sure his mom would insist on. Running into the neighbours at the park with their dog and chatting about doggie daycare, which Martin's mother would likely be into big as well. Chatting about prey drive, about the opioid-fueled significance of human-canine eye contact—which Martin has just learned about in school—and the best organic dog treats, as people settle in for the association meetings. Martin thinks hard. He thinks a dog would make he and his mother into even more of a couple.

The thought makes him feel as if his thumbs are enormous and his toes miniscule, his big head too huge for him to heft to the very park where he'd need to walk the dog. To beyond the park and far, far away.

Martin? his mother prompts.

Suck that, he says, staring at his show, though a sidelong glance tells him his mother is smiling now—as if he has cleverly provided the correct answer, the one she has in her endless wisdom known all along.

She gets up and returns with large helpings of Caribbean coconut gelato. He places his bowl on his thighs and his skin shrivels.

Martin, she says, and pops her spoon in her mouth—and spends a long time getting that ice cream down. I'm glad you're happy, Martin, she says when she is done. Her eyes behind her glasses are fog and steel. Her smile says she knows, she knows, has always known.

Knows what? A jagged impatience rips Martin's chest. His hands seem like a monsters' cupping the sides of his bowl. He thinks that tomorrow morning, when he stands next to the height measurement taped beside his bedroom door, he will discover he has cleared five-ten, a spurt of twelve inches, at least. Could be—when she's not hunched over like she's bearing the weight of the world, his mother is tall and broad shouldered and his dad is too. Once upon a time Martin's parents could have passed for twins, Martin is sure, when his mother was more lean from not working so hard and being unable to work out. A time when his mother and dumb father saw eye to eye, sort of, when his mother would shut her books and rub Martin's dad's shoulders, sore from playing a gig half the night long while she studied, and she'd cook him pancakes and feed Martin some too. A time which Martin only dimly remembers.

Martin's mother is now frowning at him.

Martin thinks harder than he ever has as he continues to stare at his mother's soft, shapeless face. If she thinks she knows he is happy, then what has she ever really known?

Martin, she says. Why are you looking at me like that?

Science camp ends. School will start soon and Martin cannot fucking wait, sorry-not-sorry. He runs algorithms, watches his shows, visits his cats. Despite his mother's mushrooming Post-its—NO! INCORRECT! HERE CROOKED FIX!—fewer workmen arrive each day and some days no one shows. Martin evilly considers writing his own notes and sticking them everywhere, a single repeating phrase he imagines used by people working black rotary phones in vintage movies. TO WHOM DO YOU WISH TO SPEAK? It's similar to what his mother says on her phone at night in her bedroom, in secret still keeping the world safe. Or so she claims, it occurs to Martin. TO WHOM AM I SPEAKING? He decides against it. These days his mother is crabby with him for not emptying the dishwasher or picking up his used towels. She makes him microwave his own food. She microwaves her own and takes it upstairs and shuts her door behind her.

School begins at last and Martin feels killer happy. Until one night during the third week of September his mother mutes the TV in the middle of Martin's show. She would like to take him for a ten-day excursion to the Bahamas, over Thanksgiving. He'll need to miss some classes.

Martin's favourite criminal jumps up and down and appears to spout zingers that come-up everyone, and which Martin is now missing. He stares and stares at the screen. What's his pal saying?

Martin, his mother says. I am speaking to you. Please respond.

Searching for correct response. Unable to locate correct response. Okay, Martin says. Ha ha.

It's when I can get time off, Martin, his mother says in that crisp, keeping-it-together voice of hers, the one she used to unleash on the dad-o. And better believe that right now I can get one smart package deal, she continues. Doesn't that sound like a good idea? Like a whole lot of fun? Martin?

Sounds fucking bat-shit, Martin says calmly, gaze still averted.

She presses unmute on the remote and they watch the rest of the show in silence. The show ends and Martin scratches his knee and his mother clicks off the TV and sits tight as Martin's lid, the one he keeps tight on his big fucking head. And then somehow the remote is in his hand, his giant hand. As if it's no longer attached to his still-puny kid's arm, his hand jerks and the remote crashes into his TV tray. Batteries explode out, bouncing and rolling. His glass of lemonade tips over.

Martin's mother flinches, her smile soured. I'm worried about you, Martin, she says quietly.

Martin feels his face flush. He is fucking eleven. What does she want from him? Yeah, he says uncertainly, voice cracking. Well, I'm worried about you.

Her face convulses. Yeah? she says, twisting the word to an ugly sneer. You mean yes? she says. As in, yes you know I'm worried? And why would you worry about me? You think you know a lot, don't you?

The living room seems vast, bottomless. Martin's feet seem to swim and swell before his eyes. He has the odd, panicked thought he should try to catch them before they get away. Yeah, he says again, louder this time. And you don't? Think you know everything?

She stops speaking to him for a few days and then it is mostly business as usual. How was school? Will that be Wasabi Warrior or Sweet Ginger Soy? She preps his pot stickers and they eat by the TV again. By late October she complains to Martin that the financial dude neighbour has turned the other townhouse owners against her. They barely say hello. They've stopped responding to her calls for association meetings. They excluded her—and Martin too, if he can believe that, imagine doing that to a kid, she says, shaking her head—from their First Festive Fall Potluck. There goes her plan to have everyone chip in and jointly buy the easement rights to the shared guest parking lot at the end of their townhouse row—the lot adjacent Martin's and his mother's eastern end-of-group, and the rights to which are held by the offices for a childhood disability services organization that sit behind the townhouses. Martin's mother has taken to grooming through the lot after she gets home from work and before dinner for stray pieces of trash left, she claims, by the employees, garbage she captures in large freezer bags and labels by date as evidence. In case, she says.

Mid-November she pressures Martin to make his bed in the mornings. One morning, she threatens to withhold his allowance for the rest of the month when he hits his head on his bed frame and swears. Which, he protests, would not have happened had she not forced him to make his stupid—her word—bed. I'm sorry my bed is so stupid, he finishes the argument by yelling lamely, and swats a stray tear from his cheek. A tear for which he swears to loathe her forever and a day.

For Thanksgiving, instead of a Bahamian cruise Martin and his mother join her North Sider sister and brother and their families at the brother's Irving Park house, as they have for the past few years. Martin sits crammed in at a far end of the table from his mother and picks at his turkey. His cousins, seated next to Martin, are too young for anything but terrible fart jokes. His mother, at the opposite end of the table, listens expressionlessly while her brother, who is an architect, ridicules the layout of Martin and his mother's townhouse, criticizes the construction materials and finishings he saw on his only visit, hating to make the trip to the South Side. Martin's aunts and other uncle attend to their innocent, stupid brats and it occurs to Martin that once again he and his mother are a childless couple set apart from the crowd.

When dessert finally comes, Martin devours several slices of the pumpkin and apple pies his mother bought at the organic supermarket. His blood uncle cracks a few unkind jokes in Martin's direction about growing men, at which his mother chins up and stares above her brother's head. She looks like she has smelled a terrible fart, not just heard some bad jokes about them, and is taking the high road, as she often counsels Martin to do.

For the first time, Martin feels badly for her. Despite the grudges he holds over her recent general moodiness toward him, he suddenly longs to throw his arms around her as he used to when he was much smaller, when she was studying through dinner, through weekends, through his dad's frequent absences, and she'd momentarily close her books and laptop and offer her bracing smile.

Martin pushes his empty plate away and knocks back his glass of milk. He calls out the length of the table, past the unkind adults and dopey kids, to his mother. Mom, he says. Mom?

She pushes her own plate away, leaving her pie half eaten. She coughs loudly and raps the table with her knuckles. The aunts and uncles and cousins go quiet. Martin quickly feels ashamed of having felt badly on her behalf, as if this might weaken her.

Martin? she says. I believe Martin would like to say something.

The aunts and uncles and cousins all turn to look at Martin. He clutches his stomach with both arms and rocks forward. Mom, he groans, facing into the white tablecloth. Mom, I have a stomach ache.

His blood uncle grunts and shakes his fat head. The aunts try to hide their smiles. Martin's cousins gum their pie innocently in his direction, whipped cream streaking their noses.

Martin's mother dabs her mouth with her napkin and drapes it on the table. She regards everyone solemnly, as if making a crucial determination. Then her gaze falls on

Martin and she smiles as if she has found the very thing that will set everything straight. Let's get you home, she says, eyebrows arched knowingly as she over-carefully articulates each word.

Martin's mother drives slowly through his uncle's nearly traffic-less neighbourhood. She misses all the lights. It's snowing and Martin has his window buzzed down a few inches. Frigid air and the occasional flake wash in. Eventually, the impressive buildings of Lakeshore Drive swim coolly, serenely into view. Some of the high-rise apartments are lit like aquariums and Martin thinks of the people in those rooms, paddling around in lives they maybe can't leave. Some units are dark as if the people in them have drowned or not yet paddled forth from their mother's insides.

Martin? his mother says after several minutes of cruising among the few vehicles out at this time. I asked you to do something. The window, please. Up.

He ignores her. He can barely remember the old apartment in which he was a baby and then a little kid and then an older one. The chipped-enamel stove, stained bathroom sink, the sound of his dad's razor tapping against the porcelain when he rinsed it of stubble—these memories and more ripple and evaporate. Martin thinks his way toward the townhouse, mapped with his mother's Post-its toward some future perfection only she can see. He can only see parts of his own future, like shooting as tall as his parents. Like leaving the townhouse, the city, off to college.

Then what.

Martin, his mother says. Do as I tell you.

Or what. He slumps further in the passenger seat. The future, he thinks glumly, is as far away as the past.

And then it is not—Martin's mother lifts her hands from the wheel and jerks her head toward him. Listen to me, she snaps, and the car strays into the left lane.

Mom, he cries.

She rights the car and stares straight ahead. What's going on? she asks after a moment, voice again practiced and smooth.

Something thin and sharp rises within him. Buzz it up yourself, he tells her, voice as calm and precise as hers. You have the controls on your side, he tells her.

That's not the point, Martin, she says after another pause. Work with me on this.

Sorry-not-sorry, he says in his new voice. You can do and say whatever you want. Just leave me out of it.

At home Martin continues to feed the cats. He cleans their litter. He plays with them in the first-floor bathroom after school and on weekends. Hello kitties, he says. He tells them his best fart jokes. Each time he leaves, he closes the door carefully so the cats won't escape. Bye for now, kiddos, he says.

Public Storage Available Now

Inside the Queen's Little Queen.

Butter.

A toy syringe.

Three Cheerios.

Clot of red thread from the Dowager's tin sewing kit.

A darning needle—the Queen's Little Queen bites back a gasp—blackened under a votive flame's sizzle then withdrawn at the last second.

Wider, the Queen commands, holding each object high and pronouncing on it before undertaking the insertion. The Queen's Little Queen's thighs quake—that's our girl, big baby at fifteen, *la petite ami*. Stocked and restocked this past hour.

A yellow button for the Queen's beloved granny in hospice since last week.

Blue for errant dadster ensconced this past month in a downtown love pad with his hottie-in-waiting. For her a tube of orange-flavoured Bonne Bell lip gloss.

A bed sheet canopies the ceiling over the rarely used basement cocktail bar. Cut-out camels and albino elephants from *National G*, affixed to the sheet with safety pins, sway and flicker in the candlelight. There's a Versailles ripped from a history textbook. Paper rubies from who knows. A *Beautiful Homes* photo of a glossy armoire carved with toucans and vines and monkeys chattering of rumoured tiny and tinier ivory-inlaid drawers. The Queen's Little Queen, delirium ravaged, imagines cubby upon cubby stuffed with treasure. In one drawer, a miniature Queen's Little Queen—our girl, all cunt.

Break time. The Queens ascend the basement stairs to swig grape sodas in the dinky kitchen. Everything is dated avocado, very barf but the Dowager's money doesn't grow on trees. She's out wrapping raw steaks and chicken legs at the A&P so she can return long past dark bearing Hamburger Helper, shredded pink flesh, pineapple juice in a can. A carton of chocolate milk to wheedle into the Little One who usually refuses sustenance heartier than crackers and *Cagney & Lacey* reruns during evening visits. Yesterday's morsel of dead ant from her own so-called home's driveway doesn't count. Nor do the thimblefuls of Liquid Plumber she's begun to imagine.

The Little Friend, her teachers have long called her. The Goer-Alonger, her own mother carps. Mother Rat, is how the girl thinks of the woman. Mother-Hunk of Spoilt Ham.

But here and now our girl is the Queen's Little Queen, sloshing the soda in her can. Make it last, she prays. But the Queen—desperate to avenge the recent disintegration of her realm, an apple blush spreading on her furious cheeks—crushes her empty bare handed and flips it into the sink. She claps twice. *Tu! Vite!*

Hurts more this time. The Queen's Little Queen's tender tissues burn.

Inside her, knuckles like newts from a spell, a headful of smoke.

And silent prayer—Tale of No Time to Speak. Word buzz, a whole ball of wax.

She shortcuts home across her school's football field, a pasture of bright heavens above. *Je suis*, she reminds herself. *Tu es.* French test tomorrow. Anything to take her mind off.

Like Tale of Once Upon a Time—news from the world at large, which she has learned at school—Some Immortal Sparks Fell. A plane burst over a place called Lockerbie. Or a plane plunged into the Sea of Japan, or more recently the Indian Ocean. She imagines the human cargos screaming like the legions of classmates cartwheeling their game-days' silver and purple, frantically displaying their hearts of shaking pom-poms.

Flight—failed, cast-down—is where the Queen's Little Queen's mind most roams.

Late again. Our poor girl! We feel for her. We do. She'll be late for her own funeral. Little Miss Dirty Little Can't Hack It Go-er Alonger, whatcmerensaythat. Locked in her bedroom at this sorry excuse for her own home, she attempts to drown out Ranting Mom with vintage *Bang a*

Gong. There's also her AP English paper, due nine sharp tomorrow morning. Get it on. *Paradise Lost*, she keystrokes at the top of page one.

Middle of the night, sick of the racket—and needing a break from spiriting into existence another A—our girl climbs through her first-floor bedroom window. She's off to the Queen's. Where else can she go? Leaves sharpen on the wind and she bucks across the frost field craving bacon, toast while dim satellites swarm among even fainter stars. She has in her knapsack two decent pages of her essay on Miltonic inversions to light her path. She has, deep in her cortex, what she thinks of as her magic pen.

She lets herself in with her spare key and camps out in the kitchen. Come dawn the paper's done. Enter the Dowager. She stands in her nightie, grey bangs mopped to one side of her crumpled-looking head.

Oh, it's you, Little One!

C'est moi!

A chuck from the Dowager beneath the chin—positively golden. Then exit the Dowager to prepare for another eleven-hour shift stickering and shelving goods.

Enter the Queen. Who two weeks ago—and unknown to the Dowager—quit tenth grade. The Queen scrabbles through the back of the freezer. *Voilà* vodka, which she dresses with o.j. from concentrate. Then she refills the bottle with tap water.

Exit the Dowager through the front door, quick-quick.

In the basement the Queen bends once more to her task. Quick-quick the Queen's Little Queen's head smokes again. More prayer—for making it to third-period French. For Tale of Toking Up With Alan and Soledad—remember them, our girl's less fucked-up friends?—Behind the Portables Before Lunch. Tale of *Je ne me reviens pas au revoir.*

Suddenly the Queen withdraws her hand with a jerk. What have we here? she says. What's the meaning of this?

Meaning? Confused, the Queen's Little Queen thinks of her paper—Tale of Tiny God of Little Gods, Tale of Work Abandoned—with its delicious hair-splittings laid out cold upstairs on the kitchen table.

Answer, the Queen demands, and the Queen's Little Queen lifts her head and twitches her legs. She muddles a hand between her thighs. Oh that.

Tale of the Late Bloomer, Commencer Finally of Her First Menses, Tale of—

Nothing, she murmurs in response to the Queen's outrage.

Another tale comes to mind. *Étant donnés*. Given States. Recently learned about in art class. An assemblage wrought in secret for twenty years. It now resides in a museum, on display for all. Viewers sidle up to a wooden door and peer through a peephole. In the foreground, a life-sized simulacrum of a dead naked woman lies spread-eagle on a bed of dead twigs and leaves. She holds a gas lamp in her left hand and the light shines toward a pleasant wooded landscape.

Rien, the Queen's Little Queen silently, ferociously

vows. For it is here that she feels for us. Our Girl! Tale of Nothing She Will Not Go On To Do.

Empress. Tale of *s'ïl vous plait nous parler.* Talk to Us. Light Our Way.

Death and the Maidens

He is seven or six or twelve. The sack he carries bulges and shrinks. He is Isidore, not yet Edwin. The sack squawks and pummels his leg.

I'll give you twenty cents for those chickens, a woman calls across the narrow street.

She shades her eyes with a wrinkled hand. Her hair sticks out in stiff grey wires. She is not his grandmother who looks after him. She is not his mother who does not.

A peck on his leg near his rear end reminds him—walk. Eight more blocks but the butcher pays better. Upon Isidore's return, his grandfather will count each nickel and cent, telling the sum in his palm with a finger. When he is done, he will tally again.

The woman pats beside her on the stoop. She rocks from side to side. Little boy, she croons.

No, Isidore thinks, continuing on, kicking stones and stamping the cracked sidewalk with his tight shoes. His grandmother might buy him only one new-used pair a year, before school starts, but he knows right from wrong. It's like a sum he can do in his head.

Jew boy, the woman cackles behind him.

Another journey. On this one, he is not near-wronged but dead wrong.

No, he says anyway, and stamps his foot. To his surprise, it is bare. The boat rocks and water sloshes in. Reeds rustle, oars dip though no rower is visible. A tall green bird lifts overhead. Its thin legs dangle. In a blink the sky blacks and stars course the complicated channels above, below. He rattles the wooden locket tied around his neck with string. As if that will help. His wife, daughter, son hole up inside. No! He wants to go back. Why can't he go back?

He snaps hands to hips and fumes until the breath whistles through his nose. Ida and Bernice and Abraham and Samuel and Meyer. Isidore, until Uncle Abe—one-seventh part-owner of a racehorse, one-third co-owner of a three-taxi fleet, bootlegger, donor to the sole shul of Saint John, New Brunswick—rolls up his sleeves. The transformation occurs in a shabby room at city hall. Edwin. No more schoolyard taunts until he dizzies like a girl. No more nightmares or his grandfather's failed attempts at exorcising them, swinging aloft a chicken by its legs and praying once in Hebrew, three times in Yiddish before chopping off the head with an axe. Worked for the man nearly hit by a falling piano on moving day. Worked for the girl who watched her sister drown in the Saint John River one sunny afternoon. Isidore-now-Edwin's grandfather charges fifty cents apiece, extortionate rates, but so long fear of the murdered who got left behind in the old country, fear of income tax in the new. The old man hears it all and swings the bird and the fright flies out—good riddance—then he counts and recounts the sums, standing by the kitchen's wood stove. He also peddles pots and pans, driving his horse-drawn cart alongside Saint John's increasing numbers of cars and buses and trucks. He stands arms folded next to his friend Morris in the back of the synagogue every Shabbas eve and loudly takes issue with the Rabbi's discussion of the Torah portion.

The old ways.

Eddie-once-Edwin-once-Isidore will abandon them of course. For a high school dance with blonde Julie Ross. Nine months at business college and an office job among skinflint Scotch Presbyterians. Tommy Dorsey on the car radio. Montreal when the employer opens an office there and Oscar Peterson in tiny clubs after work and—so open-minded is Eddie—all manner of prostitutes. Until Eddie marries a chesty brunette he meets at the High Anglican wedding of a pal back home down east.

She converts. No easy feat in Saint John in those days. But as luck would have it, a young and progressive Rabbi visiting for the winter from New Jersey permits her to study with him. Not that she has a religious bone in her body—neither does Eddie. She converts for his remote, orthodox father's not-quite acceptance. For her ticket out of fearsome Saint John, where she grew up in a house with no indoor plumbing, sharing a single outhouse through vicious Maritime winters with seven older brothers and one older sister and one gut-twitchy ghost of a dead eldest sister, passed at age twelve from acute appendicitis and a thirty-mile drive in the middle of the night from the family's outskirts home to the nearest hospital, only to arrive too late. Goodbye, Eddie's bride bids her alcoholic communist Canadian Railway union-organizer father. Farewell, recent memories of her diabetic mother who stopped taking care of herself since the death of her first-born girl and who herself dies a year before her youngest daughter's Jewish wedding. *Jew*-ish, is how the Scotch-English brothers and sister and father pronounce the word. So long to all that small mindedness.

And so to Montreal where the couple roosts. And soon thereafter another transfer, to Toronto, where the baby girl is born. Sinatra on the radio. Frequent business trips to New York and all manner of kicky hookers sporting coral-coloured lipstick, Eddie's favourite. Which he tries to talk his wife into wearing each time he returns home.

High hopes for his girl though. Supreme Court judge, heart surgeon. He loves her so much. Each workday morning he straightens his tie in the kitchen while the toddler perches in her high chair at the newly bought dinette set and molests a soft-boiled egg. Who's your handsome papa? he asks and his wife tsks. You! he trains the kid to gurgle. Smart like papa.

When she turns four—pretty as a princess—he takes her to visit her handsome papa's office.

It is Saturday morning. His wife is home, miserably pregnant again. Eddie plants shorty in his desk chair where she can study the desk calendar featuring naked ladies while he telexes Denmark, Greece, Hong Kong. He takes her to lunch and flirts with the waitresses who tease him about his miniature girlfriend. He orders her strawberry shortcake and after her first two mouthfuls tells her she better watch her figure. He likes his ladies slim.

Sometimes as the girl grows bigger he juts hands to hips and cuts her off in the hallway or a corner of the living room. Or he lies in wait for her outside the bathroom door. Who's your handsome papa? he demands as if posing a math question or quizzing her on her Prime Ministers.

John Wayne. Ol' Blue Eyes and Dean. Ain't that a kick in the pants? How the girl grows. And the mouth on her. What did you say, smart-mouth? Does someone need a good swift one? Don't make me take my belt off.

Christ's sake. The boat again. Nearly forgot. Where is he? Where was he? His wife. Not of his family's faith but she converted—and boy did she cost him. Not cheap the hair and make-up and smart plaid pedal pushers and Jesus the hats. Starting with all the debt she'd acquired before the marriage, but he bailed her out. And then the newlywed needs—maple-veneer dresser set, navy Samsonite-luggage set. The loan with interest, never repaid, to her second-youngest brother the fired bank manager. Birthdays and Mother's Day mother-of-pearl earrings and twelve-karat bracelet charms—Sears' semi-best. Her biannual threats of divorce, venomous enough to scare the daylights out of Eddie. Did she ever cost him. On the eighth anniversary of her death, he tells his daughter this, wanting to believe they're still close. Wanting her forgiveness, wanting her to understand him.

He can see from her face she's angry or worse.

What did he do? Just tell him.

Already this is years ago. But he stamps his foot in the boat just thinking about it and another foot of water crests in. How's that for a kick in the pants? After all he has done. The sacrifices. Scrimping to save for this brat's education—and she refused science, turned up her nose at law. How can he understand? His daughter with her fierce loyalty to her bitter mother. That unhappy woman. Would it have hurt her to smile more? Like his own mother, who could not afford to raise him—unexpected youngest of five—and who entrusted his upbringing instead to his paternal grandparents. Okay, he can try to understand that. But how comprehend this? In the early days of Eddie's marriage, when his own mother lay dying in a Saint John hospital bed—when he'd driven through the night from Montreal to see her and entered the hospital room—she lifted her worn head with its white hair like wires from the pillow to say, What are you doing here?

What is he doing here?

Where was he?

Eddie, Edwin, Isidore. Aunt Mary, wife or sister to Abe—the truth forever lost to the silence that enshrouds new-immigrant make-do—spoils the boy rotten. A new leather belt with a shiny belt buckle. A pair of creased seersucker shorts. Who's the handsome little man? Who is never invited to the birthday parties of the rich Jews across the river, the ones who hold birthday parties. Boy who one afternoon returns from school to his grandfather's house to find the police dismantling the backyard still. They arrest this enterprising Talmudic expert and small-time peddler. Born to a Lithuanian village once renowned for its Rabbinic scholars and a store of customs including exorcism—a village in which there now exists no record of Jews ever having lived, let alone thrived. Dirty bootlegging Jew. Most likely the police release Eddie's formidable grandfather soon after the arrest. But of this Eddie has no memory except that of shame stuffing him like river mud until he is choked full and shut tight around it like a green-tinged clam.

Not that he has never unburdened.

Soon after he marries, he comes clean to his wife despite his abundant strayings—as if proud of them, he tells her everything, every dirty thing he does with whoever he finds close at hand. What else are women for but for Eddie to pour himself and all his longings into? Excepting his own mother. That one. And what can his wife do about any of what he tells her? Hightail it with her lousy grade-eight education back to her lout brothers and alky father and boozing surviving sister to unforgiving shithole Saint John? Eddie continues to tell his better half of his fucks and affairs, the still and arrest and the story of his original name, and forbids her to ever tell. Not the daughter. Not the son who arrives later.

But the years of infidelity and screaming, the wedding gown shredded by her own hand and tossed to the garbage, wear on Eddie's wife. She does tell. Does she ever. Every dirty thing, every thing Eddie finds shameful about his past. Stoked with one pill after another—years of medications to ease the burdens—Eddie's wife beckons the teenaged daughter to her one day. The daughter she and the husband, united in this at least, insist on calling Daughter.

Your father, the sickened woman rages. And suddenly her long-denied and frightful past—with Eddie and long before him, another story entirely, for another time and place—flies back inside her. She battles and hurts. Your goddamned Jew father, she lashes out. Think he's so great?

When Eddie's wife dies, she dies alone. Death from heart disease, not helped by the fact she is skeletal from years of under-eating. Which for years Eddie has encouraged. Alone from years of pushing away her children with her silences and angry, scattershot paroxysms and over sharing.

The night before she passes, the hospital calls to say she is fading fast. Eddie is confused, terrified. His wife, leave him? For real? Not possible. No!

The hospital calls early the next morning. Hurry, some woman, some nurse is saying—no, a lady doctor. There's not much time, she tells him. She tells him, We're holding your wife for now, but hurry.

Instead of a taxi, Eddie calls his son who lives two hours away. Eddie's daughter lives in another country, already in her own story, one Eddie at eighty-one years of age cannot for the life of him read so he refrains from calling her. When he finally arrives at the hospital with his son, his wife is gone, may her memory be a blessing. Eddie and his son—a mother's boy, as is often the way, though not in Eddie's own case—weep in each other's arms.

Years of guilt and shame follow. Eddie could have been nicer. Could have been there. Could've-should've, he thinks, weeping at three in the mornings, four. Cocooned in a grief monumental like no other's. Oblivious that his daughter drifts in her own shit-stew—another long story—and his son drifts, but less so. There is also a grandson, an innocent, beloved by Eddie's dead wife. By Eddie once as well but whose very existence is also eclipsed by Eddie's mourning. Then suddenly remembered—the grandson screamed at days before his wedding to a biology teacher of Korean descent. Berated for the disrespect of not ordering a special dinner of salmon instead of chicken for Eddie and his new wife—Eddie having quickly remarried after his first wife's death, to help manage his guilt and shame. This new wife is of all things old-ways orthodox and yet arm-twisted by Eddie into breaking the Sabbath so she can accompany him to the Catholic wedding service on a Saturday afternoon—he refuses to attend without her and the thought of him not attending breaks her good heart though she is helpless to prevent his railing. Anyway. Any idiot knows salmon is classier than chicken. Any idiot who doesn't know—grandson or not—can kiss Eddie's ass.

The wedding, dear Lord. Koreans on one side of the reception hall, whites on the other. Eddie sputters over the remains of his fish when an old friend of his first wife pads over to pay a compliment to Eddie's daughter—Eddie angry that his daughter, in town for the wedding, keeps her back to him. The spitting image of her mother? Eddie snorts. But my first wife was beautiful, Eddie yells, so loud that couples skirting the dance floor startle. What? he yells a moment later. Just kibitzing. What, can't take a joke?

Did I ever tell you about our honeymoon? First one! First is always best. Hey, a joke, okay? Anyway we're in New Hampshire and—

There is only one photograph, which he takes. His first wife sticks out her full breasts like he tells her to. Her belly high and round. Curvy you bet. You bet she likes to eat. And skinny him—she will carry her husband over the threshold of their first apartment that first day in their new life together in Montreal.

Years later she will starve nearly to death like he tells her to. What, eating again? Stop with it already!

And then she does starve to death.

Another way of saying congestive heart failure. Another way of saying starved heart. No salmon. Certainly no chicken.

This wife dies and dies alone for nearly nine years after her death. Then her boat drifts from this story.

Somewhere in all this, Eddie's brother. Once upon a time, a Second World War hero. Ace figure skater who entertained the troops by skating in drag during war-time extravaganzas. Post-war he owns a children's shoe store, for which Eddie disparages him, this hero who once saved a torpedoed cruiser by hurtling into the engine room and fixing—something. Eddie can never remember what. Though he does experience pride when his brother is featured late in life in newspaper articles about miraculously active seniors. Get a load of this. Figure skating at age eighty-five on the rink at Toronto City Hall's Nathan Philips Square. Swimming at the Cassie Campbell Community Centre pool in Brampton at age ninety-one. Will you look at that, Eddie allows when his new wife shows him the pictures. Isn't that something?

Dear Eddie. So much to tell.

Did I ever tell you about the time? What? What's wrong with you?

Once she is grown past childhood and early adolescence, Eddie's daughter begins to understand. His love shames her. Until, entering middle age, she gives up on him. It's like she stamps her foot and clear water rushes in and washes him from her. Simple as that.

If only! Her days and nights until now have passed like queasy green flashes. The nights especially. Algal patches in which she sinks in the swamp that is her father. His story that has swamped hers.

But she does it. It's like she stamps and stamps her foot until mid-middle age, late middle age and on—until he mostly only returns to her as a mild migraine, feathery and light, that quickly lifts.

Here's a good one. From long before the lifting. Strap in. Ready?

The daughter's first girlfriend, with whom the daughter is slavishly in love, encounters Margaret. Follow?

Margaret is an older woman who lives in a condominium building that the daughter's girlfriend, who owns a security company, patrols with her assorted guard dogs, who she rotates twice-nightly out of respect for their beautiful dog bodies and minds, a respect for animals the daughter loves like crazy in her girlfriend. Anyway. The girlfriend meets Margaret. Margaret flirts with the daughter's girlfriend. Invites the girlfriend in for coffee, cake, a hummus wrap, whatever—Eddie's daughter has to piece the story together later. Figures out that yappy Margaret knew Eddie—amazing but true, some ruthless alignment of the stars, the fates conspiring, heavy karma, the daughter doesn't know what else to believe—back when he hadn't yet been forced to retire from his office job for padding his modest credit account. Seems that back then Eddie was the life of whatever party the industry got going and naturally flirted with every female around including Margaret. Who back then happened to work in the same industry. Somehow he shows up at Margaret's one night and attempts entry. And here Margaret, telling the daughter's girlfriend, clears her throat, the daughter imagines—imagining this is around the time the girlfriend tosses in with Margaret for a night or two or three. And surely, Eddie's daughter is sure, surely her girlfriend fucks Margaret's brains out. Anyhow, Eddie's daughter never does get a straight answer on certain particulars of the story—except for the general fact of the infidelity and the relating of her father's attempted infidelity—before she boots the girlfriend.

Sound familiar? Eddie's daughter tells more than asks herself, more than once.

Before finally piecing the sordid details together in the following days and months and years.

Before finally deciding to fuck this fucked lineage. And remove herself altogether from this story.

Fuck.

Anyhow. Following his first wife's burial, Eddie refuses to visit her grave until the unveiling of her headstone. Once it is unveiled he continues to refuse to visit. The grave perches atop a steep hill too tough for him to climb, he claims. But really it's that, as is customary, her marker faces east. Like all the stones around her. Like his parents and grandparents' in the old Jewish cemetery in Saint John. Old jazz. Too much to bear.

Also his first wife's marker is a double—one half inscribed with her name and the whatnot his daughter came up with. The other half is blank, waiting for Eddie's own passing. Eddie, it will say. Or Edwin-not-Isidore. Or—Eddie isn't sure what his daughter will say, what her mother told her.

Also, his first wife's headstone stares at him as do all the other markers. For shame, for shame, as his first wife's boat drifts on without him.

For eight years she drifts farther from this story and then drifts from this story but before she does, each time he rises at three-four in the morning for his matzo and jam snack, he is eighty-seven, fifty-two, thirty-five, and somehow nine and seven. He eats weeping in his new wife's kitchen then races to the bathroom where he shits all over the toilet seat.

His new wife, orthodox like Eddie's own mother who couldn't keep him, wakes and arises from the conjugal bed and cries too. The mess. She is eighty-one and eighty-two-three-five and somehow sixty-three and forty again. Her first husband Polish, a holocaust survivor. Grievously ill much of their married life, constantly requiring her care. Insisting from his sick bed that only Jewish nurses and Jewish doctors visit the house—her first husband terrified under the hands of non-Jews. And then after years of her care finally dead, may his memory be a blessing. She cries and cries. And the daughter of her new husband refuses to call. And one of the new wife's own daughters, a lesbian and living on the east coast, which might as well be another country, refuses to call.

Daughters—such trouble, such spite. For what?

Isidore, in a dress. He is three or four. Aunt Mary does it, common enough for young boys back in her day but increasingly not done, not here—the dress, the morning appointment at the portrait studio across the river on the rich side of town. She has saved and saved from her earnings at Woolworths.

The sweet child she never had. Daughter.

Irresistible, the dark hair in curls.

At least Eddie's son is not much in this story. He is spared here. He has his own story, one only he knows, while for incommunicado years his sister drifts in her own story farther from her mother and father and brother's boats. The brother's sister far along, ahead. Perhaps she has always been. First-born's curse. Different from the second-last-born's, like her mother. Different from the last-born's, like her brother, father too—who, now that thank god she has given up on him for good, is finally alone with his own story.

The night boat winds through tall water weeds. Days and days of night. The stars grow bored and give up. The moon grows lonely and gives up. The green bird lifts one last time. Eddie lies down. The boat leaks. How dare it? Christ's sake. Water hugs his shoulders and chest, tickles his ears until the water slides a consoling balaclava over his head, with holes for his eyes and nose and mouth. He looks like somebody's old babushka. True, he is ninety-four-five. His breath vapours the cold. Will he never die? If only he could kick his feet. Kick something. Christ's sake. Kiss my ass.

Isidore-not-Edwin-not-Eddie lugs a sack of chickens, his grandfather's treasures, to the butcher. A long walk. An old woman.

Jew boy, she calls after him. Dirty Jew Christ-killer.

He flinches. Another chicken pecks his leg. He is six or eleven. He is tired. Of the chickens and old women and the grandfather who will exorcise all this, this afternoon or the next.

The boy turns the corner onto a vacant street and the nasty crone disappears.

A chicken pecks a hole in the sack and the beak sticks through. It sticks the boy's rear end.

The hen will disappear soon from the boy's story and from its own story too.

Before that, the boy flicks his arm. The chickens screech. Christ's sake, the boy thinks. His first curse. Something he has heard the butcher say when flies get on the expensive lamb chops the boy fears he will never get to eat. Christ's sake. He swings his arm high. He drops the bag on the side-walk. Do those hens ever squawk. He picks up the bag and swings it again. Again he drops the bag.

This Wicked Tongue

Here beginneth a short treatise of contemplation taken from the Book of Alice Nash, Ancress of Shere, c. AD 1372[*]

Before we leave we tell You—smoke kestrel, thumb sky. But since friend Nance's murder, our words a poor magic mashed to this world. Then we are off our knees. We sneeze and admit Mam's relief at our leave taking. She wants no mob here, poxed cursers seeking to lay blame and wreak vengeance for our imagined sins. We smudge a tear from young Bea's cheek. Boy, we say to young Robert. A curtsy for Pa mute from the Long Wars. We hold back a sneeze. The sun fights a

---

* *In medieval Europe, a male anchorite or female anchoress ("ancress") was a type of religious hermit usually sealed in to a cell (an anchorhold) for the remainder of their life for the purpose of intensive spiritual devotion removed from worldly distractions. Practitioners may have believed they were helping to stabilize—to anchor—the church and society, and the sacrifice was valued during calamitous occurrences, including the Great Mortality, as the plague was then sometimes designated.*

cloud. The old donkey's nose dabbles air and he twitches his flied flank. From cousins Matilda and Joan one hill over, two quick waves. We scan the second hill, the third. No Nance.

We sling up our pack.

Wind on the mountain passes. Yesterday our feet froze and thawed and a swift hare defied a hawk. Yesterday we sang. We chopped firewood and slept strong.

Today we stumble, rock and root. Bound breasts ache. We miss Mam fretting over Bea's coarse braids, Robert tossing his cap, off to tend the ewes. We miss the ewe called Rose.

We bear on. The hold of which Nance spoke lies in Surrey, a fortnight or more southeastward. But by evening our flasks dry. Even the donkey sucks his teeth. We pray You all night.

But our pleas stir the ash and at grey light the donkey heaves. We stroke his flattened ears, lean against the sweating neck. He buckles and barks, and sad to say we coax him forward with a stick while we trod alongside, the path sour with moss. Crows rattle bare branches. Their cries banner our thin thoughts.

At high sun we sink, lick damp from rocks, pound dirt with fists. Call You with sorry sounds. Thistle girt, boat corn—we call You. But You are dark striking.

We remind You—to You we come. But You must already know. And our sorry sounds grow.

You must move us—for bless him, the donkey nips, we find our feet and soon the trees green. Violets sweet. We come to a low village where a mean tavern reeks, hurry to a ditch and drink.

For seven days and seven nights, we meet roads and winding lanes. And once, a three-legged dog with a cold searching nose the donkey does its best to bite. Where stoves blast, we beg, we eat. When Richards ask favours, we beg off. When a Margery with head scabs asks us, we head shake. Once, three robbers with sacks command us. But with three fleet axe swings, born of our seventeen hard-chore years, that's that.

We wade through fields at dusk and deers' gold scalds our eyes. Once, we spy a dead fawn by a creek, hide scaling with beetles and worms while a thrush throats.

All this Your work. O You in all things, behold we come. To You we come.

And behold, tomorrow is another day.

Eighth night. We bed by a stream, bid mild sleep as the donkey snores. And fear not for all is well, You evermore though mountains might bolt and seas surge. We tell ourselves. For as our lids grow heavy, the stream courses purple. And for each child rhyme we garble for solace, sparks spit strange sights. Crimson flocks taking flight from bleeding hills, from plague cursers wagging knives. Nance shouting, *Run, Alice, run.* And Alice did run, head gibbering like loose heavens. Until she dared halt and look back. Red halos. Cries of *Infidels.*

Run, Alice. Streaming these red thoughts.

But fear not. For all is You. The spell ends. Heavens settle, water calms. We must go far, for Nance. For You.

For now, we roll over, pretend snore in case that hastens rest. A good armpit scratch never hurt. Nor a hum to settle the chest. Soon two owls converse with the donkey's dream snorts. And all is well. Only once, a sob chokes.

O Nance.

*

She taught far and wide. Toulouse to Narbonne, Beauvais to Bruges. Low-country towns around Flanders, Brabant. A drab English shire in spring. You see all, she preached, under a stewing rain in front of the eel monger's that morning Alice first beheld her—Nance herself a miracle with cropped curls and sturdy shoulders and worldly in her knowledge and brave.

On an August afternoon, she and Alice lay together in the meadow foxtail and herd's grass which caused eye water and sneezes, but the sun streamed. Bees clustered in clover. You in all things.

In my rough heart too, Nance?

In your heart too, Alice.

Who dared draw head to Nance's browned bosom. In this, Nance?

Her chapped hand stroked Alice's neck and a breeze purred like Mam's ginger cat. This too, Alice.

Thereafter in the shade of a blackberry bush, stained lips pressing. Heat sheeting strong backs and buttocks and knees. In the season's awe light, the year swinging stout, fattening with gifts of early evening brilliants, of which Nance taught.

So much to come, we thought. For You.

On whose behalf the cursers believed they came. Early fall. West Hill where true loves Nance and Alice dallied. Kickers and stabbers, behold. You in all things.

In Nance who now lives on in Alice.

We reach a day of nights and days too numerous to tell. Swim streams, solve riddles, open gates.

At last arrive—we arrive, we tell You, in case you don't already know.

The church rubbles. As Nance had warned, describing her travels among such poverty. And so soon we beg mercy of the devout one who greets us. Who appears gaunt and confused. Neck craning, scanning to our sides, behind us. Asking, *Is there another of you?* when we put forth our case. Since when Nance died Alice became Nance too. For You.

At last, we offer all we own beyond ourselves—our poor beast as payment for scant keep. Though we are sad to see the donkey go.

At last we trip on crumbling brick and sneeze dust through dark corridors. A great door's hinges creak. Behold a dim room. Ailbertine the Tall—do You know her? We sneeze and wait while she rises from behind a desk, shakes out her black threadbares like a proud old crow.

She will think on us.

We wait on the chapel bench, splinters in our palms. We sneeze and sing songs. At last, sleep.

Next morning, Ailbertine towers. Kneel in the garden, she bids, her voice high. Tend the Lord's carrot blight.

But our donkey. In return, we must gain the cell.

But, Ailbertine says in a voice even higher. Nineteen years now Cecily holds it. What you desire you will not have. Not while Cecily lives.

We wonder, was Nance wrong? Are we?

Forgive us then, we say, figuring at least one thing fast. But with respect we request the donkey back.

Ailbertine draws ever taller. A long moment, then a withered hand grants a head prick with a long yellow claw. Bring Cecily her weekly suppers, Ailbertine commands.

Collect such body soils as might depend. Hear your Lord speak thus.

We do. For You we yank weeds and coddle weak sprouts. Fetch Cecily her gruel. Once a week, empty her chamber pan.

And do You know Cecily too? Know that one day past three weeks since we arrived, a bad pea kills her.

Know Nance was right.

At last we are on our knees by our cell's window squint. And all is well evermore, we pray You—sun spoon, blue bake.

Until a spider webs her prey by the inner casement and with her enterprise our hunger swells. Bless us—we have defecated but twice this first month.

We stand and the flagstones spin. Nance in her green dress lies down, and we lie too.

Is Nance not gone?

A feathered crow alights the outer casement of our cell's window and beaks a stone. Cecily, returning?

We lick dry lips and wonder. Is this how You speak? Between the living and the dead? On a hill, spiralling like Bea's beloved toy top, where cousins Joan and Matilda start up. And Alice among them with Mam and Pa.

We wonder. If Nance in her green dress still lies down, can Alice lie too, lie yet with Nance? Or must we continue to *run, Alice, run*. Until like a top we too twist to fog.

And Cecily, does she walk, might she return, in what state? A pea for a pea in a pale shivery hand?

Alone, nowhere else to go, we ask and ask our questions.

Maybe You don't know.

A day, a night, another day or more. At last the spell clears. We kneel again in our cell—so low, dirt humbles our lips. But our hunger gains teeth and nails and slinks.

Forgive this. Forgive this. And nothing else.

On a night of nights too long to tell, key and lock and door scrape. Behold Ailbertine bearing a torch. Bless, she squeaks.

We hop in place, clap hands to warm, sneeze. In the torchlight a smile crooks the woman's mouth like a hook. We'd almost forgotten such highness. Bless, we sneer back.

She steps closer and we get three head cuffs. One sharp kiss, which stinks of rancid meat. Our heart hammers for our old braying beast.

You spared us for this? And the weekly oatcake. The swig of water. Coins sometimes tossed at our squint by pilgrims seeking counsel. Let the light scald your eyes, we bid them. Angered, some ask for their coins' return.

Yes, bless, Ailbertine squawks. The old rich silversmith and his young love. Their sickly child. Thus put your nonsense to Godly use, or suffer casting back into the world.

Where Nance lies down and Alice lies too? And all is well evermore. Until all is not.

Or remain here, where for her passion, poor Cecily met an inglorious end. For which we truly repent. Her end we could meet too. For love of You?

Run, Nance shouts.

Let the light scald Your eyes.

Now we reach a day of days too pitiful to tell. At last a beach by a cliff. We crouch against a rock for hours, let terns tangle our hair, pull the wool from our cloak. Scavenging the water's edge for a time near nightfall, a woman in black rags like an old crow, but not one we know. For a time, we toe freeze in salt suck. Then knee and hip with breath catch, stones tied to our hem. Until neck soak, when in between sudden sneezes we face tilt. And behold the star bones of sky heroes revealed by bold true Nance.

A boulder beyond wave's reach shelters our coldest night.

Next day, old crow from the night before, with a big steaming pot.

Sage moan, cape band. Sea cave and blanket and tide. Gulps of gull soup. When darkness tucks around us, we touch ourselves to sleep. Fetch terns' eggs with each dawn. On clear evenings beneath the Mariner's brights, we dare point to the skies as Nance once did.

Constellations never before told. Here, Taker of Biddy Tolls in Wayfarer Tales. There, Digger of Fine Dusts for Scents. And here, Maker of Dab Purses, Best Baker of Delicate Loaves. There, Measurer of the Village Wells.

Another night now. Before we leave again we tell You, behold. Here, Keeper in Her Lighthouse Several Borders North. Above You, Sailor in Her Star Throne—in a time not yet come. But just You wait.

Is this how we speak? Can You hear? Simple Alice, who Nance loved. Hear how we are Nance too.

Princess Gates

The old woman came out in her nightie, went around back, returned with a ladder.

In the tree, the cat was high up, stuck, yowling.

Streetlamp, tree, streetlamp, tree. Like a picket fence around the neighbourhood.

All the young couple could do, being young, was wring their hands and run them over each other. Their cat liked to climb down from their second-floor balcony and roam.

Marguerite, Bryce. They had quite a lot of sex in those days—every day, and quite a few times every day. And fights and drinks.

The old woman, the landlady, wasn't beautiful—though her husband's name was Sweet Daddy. He'd been a pro wrestler. When Marguerite and Bryce were kids they'd seen him in county arenas, cottage country, working the crowds. Now he was old and fronted an alt-country band—*Cocaine, cocaine* lolloping from the basement in the middle of afternoons.

The old woman was the old woman who rescued the cat. Marguerite and Bryce loved the cat. Loved.

There were some neo-Nazis who lived nearby but the young couple paid no mind. Sometimes there were protests but Marguerite and Bryce were busy. She washed dishes one night in a pricey joint, broke a tray of Rosenthal. Otherwise, when she waited tables, he'd wait in the apartment, eking out crossword puzzles, hot-kniving hash, waiting for her to get home. When she did, he'd stab his fingers through her purse for cash he'd pay the cab driver with, the liquor-store cashier. Bryce bought the best, regardless of cost.

She'd been pregnant when they first met. She never thought to wonder why he didn't mind. She was busy with school, work. Her own daddy, mother.

Marguerite took care of things.

There was a lake. Cold, blue. They lived that one whole winter-spring by the fairgrounds. She tried riding a bike, a beater, through the western gates once. They were named after a princess.

The wind was a violence so she had to turn back.

One night Bryce fell. Bang went his head on the ice. Marguerite continued on her way. There were stars but no moon so the light pricked. At the edge of the parkette she stopped. Full stop. She meant it—him. Groaning, Marguerite, Marguerite. She meant it—her.

She got thin. Beautiful in that thin kind of way. Thin as her mother in her seventies would get, years later, tubes stuck in her, congestive heart failure caused by decades of refusing to eat, refusing, fuck you, so long, goodbye.

Hey, Beauty. Here, Beauty Beauty.

But look what this young woman could do. I'm leaving, she one day up and said.

Next. Next.

She has never wanted to return. Not to anything or anyone.

An older woman in a white gown. Streetlamp. Marguerite can hardly stand it. Bike, ice, lake. Bang.

Cat—dead now, right? And young Bryce, bent inside her but she hadn't minded.

What she has ever really wanted to say has been later.

As Such

Martin sinks into the plush red velvet and waits for Will to follow suit. After they settle, after the house lights go down and the conductor strides on stage to warm applause, Martin takes Will's hand. They are in Budapest. Will is having a work premiered. The hall is an intimate gilt affair and Martin and Will are seated by the aisle, four rows from the front so Will can leap the stairs onto the stage for his bow. Martin squares his shoulders, spreads his legs so he can graze Will's knee. The first movement, *allegro*, clips smartly along. During the second movement, *allegro furioso*, Will's fingers death-grip. Martin guesses it's a late entry of the crotales or maybe a muddy imbalance between woodwinds and string—the kinds of marrings that Will has with limited success trained Martin to hear. Post-performance, though, he never fails to resoundingly deny the existence of such flaws.

Will's hand-crunching crescendos. Martin nudges and Will lets go. Sorry, he mouths.

Martin smiles. He gets it. Precision, finesse. No mistakes. He and Will have been married four years now, together a total of fourteen, having met in a first-year astronomy course. The prof miscalculated a formula on the board one day and as class finished Martin and Will tripped over each other, veering forth with the correction. Martin and Will refer to the episode as their origin story.

A hush and the final movement begins. *Presto*, it says in the program. All these sparkly notes—where do they come from? Will sometimes fields such questions from civilians, as he calls people without his lifelong training and expertise. He has patient, gracious answers. Even so, Martin declines to ask. Not that it matters. The performance tonight is one great flying contraption of fast and faster and though Martin doesn't speak the language it makes some kind of sense to him. Theme, development, tension, tension. At the moment Martin's not sure where it's all going but that's okay, he's with it. He trusts. No matter that Martin's hearing isn't great—all those childhood ear infections—and he knows little of music, despite Will's insistence that Martin knows more than he admits. What counts is that Martin rely on Will's held or loose breath, clenched or relaxed muscles, the practiced ways in which two people really know each other, to tell how things are going and gone. And then the piece ends and the audience applauds solidly if not wildly and the conductor beckons. Will stands on stage and bows. He clasps his hands together and shakes them above his head at the musicians, the audience, Martin, thank *you*, bravo.

After the performance, Martin and Will sit outdoors at a crowded café and eat traditional chimney cake—an alarming construction and shudderingly sugary but they feast anyway and sip from tiny cordial glasses in honour of culinary history and the mostly successful premiere. Will smudges away a dollop of cream on Martin's face and any worry he's felt, the nameless sticky dread he often wakes to in the middle of the night, unglues. Look at them, Martin thinks. Their luck. Hard work rewarded, unlike so many people's. Tomorrow they will tour Trinity Square and the thirteenth-century Matthias Church. Visit more cafés, drink the thick coffee. After a few days they will return home to the show-stopper house they had built in a leafy Atlanta suburb. Upon slumbering ten hours a night for three nights, with any luck—insomnia on its own vacation for once—Martin will return to his lab at the university, although it is late May and officially summer break. He'll pack his modest lunches and eat in front of his computer screens. Bliss. Never mind the hard work. He thanks his sheer dumb luck.

He places his fork on the shared plate. He pushes his empty glass away and the waiter by the café door catches Martin's eye. No thanks, Martin nods. He raises his hands and pushes the air, done.

Not bliss, the sudden gouging splinter in his mind. Or, more precisely, what he thinks of as the mind of his discarded and resentful ghost flesh. The old flesh he sloughed. The overlarge boy-self that sometimes parks on Martin's chest and refuses to budge.

Fuck you, the kiddo says. Fuck everything.

To whom are you speaking? Martin silently back-talks it, as he's trained himself to do. At the same time he tries hard to think kind thoughts, to not succumb to the fat-shaming he sometimes heaps on this child Martin used to be.

As if to prove a point, Martin takes up his fork again and allows himself a morsel more.

After the nightmare of racing through the Brussels airport to make their connection, after Will as usual is the brown man pulled aside for a security interview in a windowless room while Martin frets and curses—followed by the near torture of missing their connection and exhaustedly dozing in the corporate airport hotel room they'd been forced to take, and missing dinner and then rising at four the next morning for their new flight—they arrive home sweet home. When they rise refreshed from their bed, Will pops popcorn in the microwave, Martin pours the Vouvray. They stream some flick, no big deal, and Martin enjoys the undemanding pace. He makes sure that it's Will who polishes off the few remaining pieces of popcorn. Outside the living-room window, the birch and Japanese maples and dogwood—and the peonies! like giant coral-coloured gods, some of the exquisite, costly landscaping Martin and Will had put in—nose the currents of the night sky. The plantings with their swaying remind Martin of the oceans whose graceful and imperiled inhabitants he's imagined each of the multiple times he and Will have crossed and re-crossed for getaways and conferences and performances. This place, this home, is their private Eden.

Martin collects the wine glasses and heads for the kitchen. What can I get you? he asks over his shoulder.

Don't make me say it, Will says.

Martin puts the glasses down too hard on the kitchen counter, breaking the base off one. For the past six months, Will has been after Martin. Will wants a baby. He's done all this research. Apparently he means it. A baby? A baby? Shit, Martin says. Fuck.

You okay in there?

Martin disposes of the broken stemware and returns to the living room, where Will has opened his laptop. Martin sits in the easy chair opposite the sofa. What are you doing? he asks.

Will clicks and smiles at something on screen. What are you? he says.

Fuck, Martin says.

Will's attention never wavers from his computer. Excuse me? he says.

Nothing.

Good, Will says, typing quickly. Without looking up he says, Your mother hearts the one with you in front of the Great Synagogue.

Martin wishes Will would check in with Martin's mother Top Secret and leave Martin out of it. He wishes Will wouldn't post their travel photos for Martin's mother to browse. But he feels powerless to stop Will. In the four years since the wedding, Will has acquired certain non-musical super powers with which to charm Martin's terror of a psych-doc mother, still resident in his natal Chicago. Will's math-head niece and her latest prize-winning conquests, his older brother making Assistant District Attorney for Delaware, the restaurant downtown Will and Martin recently tried—any such news does the trick. Martin's mother's voice ascends to the sprightly caprice Martin hears when Will forcibly hands a helpless Martin the phone. Why, Martin sometimes wonders, can't he admit to Will that the cost of such wondrous abilities, and their capacity to uneasily bridge the years-long distance between Martin and his mother, is more of the sudden reappearances of the boy-shithead—the sneering, chunky know-it-all Martin used to be, who rematerializes to fossick at Martin's adult ribs.

Some bridges, Martin thinks, are best blown the fuck up and never rebuilt.

Will glances over from his laptop. Hey, sad sack, he says. Remember Budapest? He pats the couch beside him. Want to see the pics again?

Palms sweating, Martin obeys, seating himself next to Will. I remember nothing, confess nothing, Martin says, smoothing and dampening his pant legs with his now-sweaty palms.

I know, Will says, tapping, clicking. You never do. What's the story on that?

You have no idea.

Martin does know the story and it's some premium bullshit. Bullshit the reasons Martin's mother once upon a time gave for the late-night phone conversations she took in her bedroom, behind her closed door when he was growing up—her claims that she sometimes did Top Secret work for the government, which forbade her to speak about it. Probably bullshit. She worked for the VA, still does, and Martin surmises that on such evenings she'd just been the shrink on call, issuing changes to med dosages for fucked-up veterans, poor bastards unlucky enough to be under her care. Criminals, was how she'd privately, at home to Martin, refer to her patients.

So how's this for Top Fucking Secret? Martin's ongoing and profitably supported research. His fancy pants algorithms—souped-up data-in, response-out programs, super-elite editions of the machine learning that enables a robot to sally forth and avoid obstacles on a kitchen floor. A lot more bang for the buck with Martin's work though. What he does enables a mini-bot to precisely navigate an abandoned apartment block halfway across the world. A ruined bedroom that once slept five. A living room where four generations once gossiped. Scourable ruins of deranged plaster and shredded furniture and maybe coded messages that could disastrously affect the beleaguered, fragile world—Life As *We* Know It, as Martin decently tries not to think of it.

As such, Martin's work is truly important. As such, the funding never fucking ends.

A baby? How does a baby fit in all this?

In such a fucking world as this?

Black, white? Martin asks the third night home from Budapest, during dinner, Will on his case again. He gave the subject its own vacation while they were away but now apparently it's up and at it and moving way too fast. Can't we slow things down? Martin wants to say. What flavour kid are we talking? Martin says instead.

Banana, Will responds with a shrug.

Why not? That'll cost years of therapy. Big bucks.

That's what parents do, dope. It's what they're for. You should know.

The grilled chicken expands miserably, betrayingly in Martin's stomach. His head sponges acids. He can't believe Will has stooped so low. Who kidnapped Martin's gentle, kind husband and swapped in an imposter?

A wounded, sour anger—one Martin rarely feels these days and is usually able to quell—coils in his throat. Today's insight brought to you by WILL, Martin snaps. Let's hear it for WISE WILLY.

Martin sits back. The bizarre, aggrieved thought of jabbing a finger down his throat and puking onto his plate crosses his mind. DUMB FUCK, he shouts inwardly. Though he's confused as to whom this thought is addressed.

Will adopts his ironically quizzical expression, which always makes Martin feel foolish beyond words. Hello? Will says. HELLO? Calling MARTIN? I think you want to walk this one back, MARTIN. Way back.

After Will falls asleep that night Martin creeps downstairs and shuts himself in the first-floor bathroom. His mother picks up within seconds. Yes, she says. I'm here. To whom am I speaking?

Hi there, Martin begins.

Where are you? she asks.

He imagines her sitting in bed, wearing an alert expression, and Martin feels a pulse of old anger. Describe the room for me, he remembers her instructing him, trying to talk him down from his swirling anxiety when he'd call during the few trips he took with his father, who'd abandon Martin for hours on end to prowl bars and hang out with local bands in whatever bullshit towns they happened to pass through. Bullshit—one of his dad's many choice words and now, when he's agitated, Martin ruefully admits, one of his own top hundred. The trips took place after his parents' marriage cracked and before a preteen Martin cut off most contact with the guy. Even back then, Martin had the smarts to realize that one parent with issues was more than enough to deal with.

Back then, his mother's issues—her talents—lay in insinuating herself into Martin's head. Describe the room for me—so she could put herself in the room, mentally accompany him everywhere, indispensible. Insert herself into his abandonment. Offer herself as the solution, his best company, the two of them in it, in everything, together. A way to bind him to her. Keep him all up in her tangled stratagems. He and his mom—she who believes she knows most everything, able to stare uncontested at things as they are—against the flawed world, as she sees it.

As a young kid, her superiority game made him feel safe. Until it angered and sickened him and he figured out he'd had enough. Of coupledom with her. Enough of her distancing ways that estranged her, and by extension Martin, from others.

Martin? she says. I said where are you?

He's not abandoned now, he reminds himself. Not with Will in his life. Martin's life is solid. Fuck his mother's worn gambits, he thinks, even as he reaches from his perch on the toilet-seat cover to turn off the bathroom light. He's safe from her, he is. Besides, where does she think he is? He's home—home!

You first, he tells her.

Where am I, she says. Good one.

How are you? he says, deciding to skip ahead.

You have no idea, she says coolly.

Same here! Martin resists the urge to crow. After all this time, how hard and crucial it still is to resist her mental trapezes, his own trick-unicycle spokes spinning beneath them. A mad world he miraculously escaped.

Redirect, redirect, he imagines a voice saying in his head. Resistance is not futile.

I have something to tell you, he ventures, sliding the soles of his feet along the slate floor tile. The chill on his skin emboldens him to proceed with his plan—to try Will's big idea on for size by trying it out on Martin's mother. See what she can get up to with it. See how Martin himself deals. He's trying!

But it's a risk. He recognizes his emotional regression—a mild one, he's sure. But he feels pushed and prodded and unsettled in ways he hasn't since adolescence. Not so solid, he has to admit. Shaken by these arguments with Will. Though he and Will always figure shit out. They always do.

Martin's mother is still on the line.

Big news, he says, hating himself a little.

A muffled swoosh. He imagines her on the mattress, surrounded by the trash she has picked and saved from the parking-lot easement outside her townhouse—the easement for which she has for years tried in vain to buy the rights. He imagines her crumpling and smoothing and re-crumpling the offending plastic bags and candy wrappers discarded by the employees of the neighbouring child disability services who park there. Her twenty-plus-years' sworn enemies. She'd also managed to alienate herself and Martin from the other townhouse owners in their group, who had no problem with the easement and resented her near-constant plotting, the way she increasingly implied that they were fools for not taking her seriously about such weighty matters. That they'd be sorry one day.

Hello? Martin says. Now that he's at this threshold, he's anxious to step across.

Yes, she answers before he's said another word—she sounds peevish, impatient. The answer is yes.

Mom?

Why do I always have to explain myself? she says, then quickly adds, I'm sorry, you're breaking up.

Martin's phone beeps. Then silence. Punishing him. Wouldn't be the first time.

Though he knows that for better or for worse, his mother would never entirely turn from him.

Marked cognitive decline, Will reports, hopping in the car at arrivals, just back from an early fall performance in Chicago. He spent an afternoon with Martin's mother, Will's first time in the townhouse in which Martin partially grew up. Disheveled appearance, unfocused eyes, Will says. Inability to follow the conversation. Yellow sticky notes plastering her dining table and bannisters and walls. The notes say things like NOT HERE! and FIX THIS. When asked, she wouldn't or couldn't tell him for whom or what they were intended.

Martin charges onto the expressway. He slams the brakes and lays on the horn when a car tucks in front of him. He swings into the passing lane and accelerates again. He feels embarrassed, furious—exposed. TOP SECRET MY ASS, he thinks. He sucks ancient bile down his throat.

Okay, Martin says.

In Chicago the leaves might be starting to colour but here it's a humid, hot day and Will knocks up the AC. Not okay, he says. I'm telling you, this is for real.

The car tears along. Listen, Martin says. You don't know fuck-all about my mother. She's always stuck those notes over everything. They were originally meant for the workmen who were supposed to fix the place when we first moved in. Nothing ever got fixed but she kept writing the crazy anyway.

Will taps his thigh with his fingers in lieu of humming annoyingly. Martin knows. And appreciates. He's glad he can't hear the distracting rhythm beneath the racing lilt of the tires. He needs to focus. He suspects a nefarious plan to have his mother move into the guest room here and help care for the baby Will wants so badly.

Suck that, hard. Hard as Martin's brain punching his brain-roof, pow, wham. Got it all figured out, haven't you? Martin wants to yell. How come you know everything? You and my mother both, in cahoots.

And what, Martin thinks savagely, does Will even know about such things or think he knows? Only the distortions Martin's mother might proclaim. So Martin can't even trust that she's as bad off mentally as she's making herself out to be, skilled manipulator that she is.

For years growing up he believed he had some kind of cancer gene, which she apparently had him tested for as an infant. An infant! Had him thinking he'd likely die young without her constant oversight. As an adult he's had himself tested—more than several times, no joke—and guess what? No such problem, according to the medical experts.

Martin jets out of the passing lane to pass a speeding semi. Cahoots, he thinks with a measure of self disgust at having aped one of his mother's quaint, paranoiac words.

What's for real is this, Martin says. She's always been bat-shit.

More tappety-tap from Will.

Well? Martin says. Well?

I think you're going to have to face some decisions for once, Will says.

Martin has so far resisted—successfully resisted, in his view—making a decision about a baby. What's more, he possesses no qualms about neglecting to do so regarding his mother, if news of her deterioration does turn out to be true—something he'll allow for, in theory. He intends such success to continue as long as stars fly over the earth and rivers flow to the sea—cue the janky music—and The World As *We* Know It still exists in all its injurious, unequal glory. Which any spin through the news cycle on his tiny screen tells him won't be forever—don't blame him—but it will last for at least a while longer. So Martin also successfully resists the urge to slam his hands against the wheel and charge the car into the next lane and the next, the ditch, FUCK.

There's that non-budging kid-weight on his chest again. A form of family, Martin supposes. Which reminds him of his dad. Somewhere in small-town Colorado—near Steamboat, the last place the dude seemed to live, the last Martin did a search for him on the internet—is there a man who remarried and fathered new kids who might resemble Martin? Family he's never known he has? And sure as shit—to use another old-timey fave phrase of his dad's—doesn't want? Martin hasn't seen the loser since high school graduation, which he nearly missed, driving from an out-of-state gig through the night to arrive red-eyed and unshaven and growling curses at Martin and his mother through mossy teeth. For so much of Martin's life it had been Martin and his peculiar, dependably manipulative mother. Until Will, who is more than enough for Martin. Adding in Will's mostly reasonable, tolerant, smart family—give or take, because what family, Martin supposes, is truly perfect?—who Martin prides himself on getting along decently with.

I make decisions all the time, Martin says, forcing himself to speak so calmly his gut aches, though the pressure on his chest lets up. I chose you, didn't I? he continues, aiming against all hope for a charm that channels Will's usual disposition, but which Martin at heart disbelieves he himself possesses. As such, he says, trying to sound convincing, shouldn't you go a little easy?

As such? Will says, clapping his hands together in unbridled delight. My god, where do you come up with such things?

Martin shrinks. Or rather he swells with diminution, an enlarged sense of smallness. He knows full well the verbal tic derives from his stubbornly unhappy childhood. In stark contrast to his dad-fueled uses and abuses of swear words, the phrase is part of his brittle attempts to rise above, construct meaning out of chaos, blah blah insert therapy speak here.

As such, he feels ashamed at the stilted phrasing of his youth. At his infelicitous growing up. His undying resentments.

But he is unwilling to back down. To be pushed around over this matter with his mother—almost anything but this. As fucking such, he says.

Language. He winces at the sound of his mother's admonitory, eternally replicable voice in his head.

Where do you come up with this garbage? Will says. Delusional, much? Loud and clear, okay? She needs your help.

How many fucks did you give today? Will asks when they arrive home from the airport.

Please let this end, Martin thinks. This sniping that is mean as ass.

He and Will are in the kitchen. Martin is on the stepladder, changing a bulb that has just burned out. He screws in the new one, wondering what joke he might be in, and steps down.

Language, he says, trying a joke for real, given his own propensities.

Will opens the refrigerator door. Zero, he says, answering his own question. You gave zero fucks.

Martin feels a chill seep from the fridge as Will's head disappears inside. WILL, Martin wants to yell. DANGER, WILL. Is this it? Has Martin pushed Will so far?

What are you looking for? Martin says, feeling skinned, eyes raw with salt.

Carrots.

Behind the apples.

Will emerges with a lemon in each hand. He hip-shuts the fridge door and juggles them.

Martin picks up the stepladder, clanks it harder than necessary as he folds it flat. I give all the fucks in the wide fucking world, he says.

Will stops with the lemons. He holds his hands up, a yellow orb in each palm. Yeah? he says. About what?

Us.

Yeah but, Will says.

But?

We're not enough, Will says, bopping the lemons together once for each word he speaks.

Code from a bad dream, Martin thinks—though he's never dreamed, not that he's aware of. Which used to concern his mother. She'd try to trick him into more talk, with her, with another shrink. All of which he began to suspect, as he got older, that she'd weaponize, use against him. Shrink him good. At a certain point he refused.

He leans the folded stepladder against his side. He looks around the kitchen, which he's successfully prevented her from seeing for real, in person. Describe the room for me, Martin replays in his head. Though his mother has, with admirable self-restraint—or the actual forgetfulness of mental decline—never asked about the house. In his head now he tells her. The expensive backsplash and custom shelving and other bougie, privileged shit. And Will—WILL. As such, HAPPINESS.

LET THE FUCK GO, Martin begs the hunk atop his heart.

You catch that, Martin? Will says. WE'RE. NOT. ENOUGH.

No? Martin says helplessly. No?

Is she really as bad as Will claims?

Had she ever been as bad, a different type of bad, as Martin remembers?

He last saw his mother two years ago. He'd flown to Midway and steered his rental to a Hyde Park significantly more chipper than he'd remembered. A sleek new corporate hotel towered over 54th Street and an apparently decent wine bar graced the lot once owned by the failed food co-op. Crime was up, though. He'd read about it in the local news he still secretly followed after all these years. Valois' See Your Food still existed, as did Rajun Cajun. Reassured, he parked in his mother's visitor spot, noted the swept-looking easement. She buzzed him in the townhouse's front gate and the front door swung open and she embraced him as she hadn't at his Atlanta wedding, where she'd reserved her one warm hug for Will and merely shaken Martin's hand. He hadn't seen her since. Why would he? He felt awkward, standing with her on the stoop of the townhouse while she wrapped him in her arms, as if he'd only just realized he were inches taller than her and unsure where to put his nose.

Let me look at you, she said, clutching his wrists and holding him at arms' length. Unusually her nails were done, a waxy scarlet he complimented and she went curiously girlish for a second, crinkling her eyes and tittering, a hand to her mouth to hide her crooked incisors. The gray-brown mane tied back as always. A faded yellow shirt Martin recognized from his childhood. Droopy faded blue shorts, also familiar seeming. She appeared to have neither gained nor lost weight. Except for the new veins popping in her hands and arms and the skin folds around her elbows, the more deeply etched frown lines on her face, she didn't seem to have aged much since Martin was eighteen and heading off to college on the east coast.

He went upstairs with her and sat on the same couch she'd bought deeply discounted when they'd first moved in. She served him a glass of tap water. She'd recently co-authored an important paper, she told him. Very important. On medication and hallucinations. In addition to her job at the VA, she now had a teaching appointment at Northwestern. He knew, he said, Will had told him. When Martin got up and paced she smiled her smug smile. Post-its to herself—DRY CLEAN CURTAINS, CALL LARA and more—lathered the window frames, the kitchen counters and cabinets. Who was Lara? Martin didn't ask. He asked after his uncle and aunt and the cousins to whom Martin had never warmed. His mother shook her head as in DON'T ASK.

Could he go through his old stuff? he asked, papers and finger paintings she'd long ago claimed to have stored in giant plastic totes in the townhouse's attached garage. He didn't say, but what he really wanted was to recover his treasured vintage bot posters, portraits of early GOFAI, Good Old Fashioned AI—one of the few cherished parts of his past, already old when he was a kid—and frame them for his office at school. Also, acquired in his late teens, the poster from the Adler Planetarium gift shop of the Algol star system in the constellation of Perseus. Algol, in the snake-haired Gorgon's head—Gorgon in the Ancient Greek tradition, Medusa to the Romans. Head of the ghoul to early Arabic astronomers. Demon star in English. Among the brightest stars in the heavens. Among the unluckiest. Ptolemy in the second century associated Algol with violence, especially decapitation. Made sense. Medusa the serpent-haired, able to turn men to stone with the horror of her gaze, herself ended headless, slain by Perseus' sword. In an amusing coincidence that Martin had once upon a time cherished, Algol was also ALGOL—short for Algorithmic Language, the influential body of computer programming languages that enabled much of life today, and Martin's work. So he also wanted that poster for his office. He thought his super-bright students might get a kick.

His mother shook her head again.

Do you still have my things? he asked and in his precise, overcompensating voice he heard hers.

In that moment he knew she truly might have done it—purged his to-him priceless belongings. Par for the course, he thought wretchedly. As a kid, after his parents' divorce, she'd allowed Martin two beautiful Bengal cats, who he'd adored. But she'd insisted on their full-time confinement in the first-floor bathroom. For years. Until Martin left for college and she re-homed them without consulting him. He'd arrived for Thanksgiving that first semester and they'd vanished. It was his last visit with his mother until this one.

Do you? he repeated sharply on that check-in, hoping to cut through her haziness. An intentional one, he assumed. Spiteful. Though he did note her once-penetrating gaze had drifted more to fog than steel over the years. Have you got my stuff? he said, trying not to let his alarm show.

So many questions, she said. I'm tired of them.

That night two years ago now, while she slept—after the early dinner of microwaved frozen organic palak paneer and freezer-burned burritos, and her efforts to also ply him with frozen organic jelly donuts she offered to defrost in the microwave, and then the lumber past dog-walking neighbours who seemed confused about who she even was when she stopped to introduce Martin to them, followed by bedtime herbal tea concocted from several re-used and differently flavoured bags—Martin tiptoed down the stairs to peruse the garage. Clean as a whistle, a phrase his mother herself might have used. No shelves, boxes, junk. The floor immaculate enough to eat off.

The morning after Martin and Will's fight—after long dark hours of cold insomniac shoulders—Martin and Will brush their teeth side by side at the double sink in the master bathroom. You don't know me at all, Martin hazards through mouth foam, somehow unable to give it a rest.

Will spits and rinses, angles the base of his toothbrush into its charging port and meets Martin's gaze in the mirror, lips curling in contempt the way Martin's mother's do.

Martin spits. And you don't know her, he says, speaking to mirror-Will. I'll go, I'm going, but there's no point. Happy now?

Will's expression turns from disgust to one of suspicion. He breaks contact with Martin's reflection and turns toward Martin-Martin.

Now Martin stares at mirror-Martin, whose chin trembles. Whose mother loses her mind. Whose mostly gentle, kind husband wants a baby. Or what? NOT HERE! NOT YET. FIX THIS. Martin—which one?—wands his tooth brush to and fro. TO WHOM AM I SPEAKING? he silently, desperately asks.

How hard can it be? To try?

Fucking hard. But he does it—torques his neck to face Will, breaking the spell. I am not alone, Martin inwardly counsels himself. I am not in this alone.

Which he knows. He knows!

And doesn't know, not really!

This is his problem—he knows that much. That he doesn't really know when he's with Will or Martin's own barbed, barbarous boy-person. Or with that boy's mother.

And Will—how is it that he's been changing into someone else without Martin noticing? A terrible lapse, he realizes. To see Will in one way only. Classically trained pianist, accomplished creator of string quartets and works for chamber orchestras and more, fearlessly forging ahead in a field riddled with restrictions for those not of the white male variety. The tenacity. The talent, of course. But now, also, this desire for a kid and contradiction, messiness. For room in Martin's heart for his impossible mother. Will—fearless AF. Unlike Martin.

I'll see for myself, okay? he says. Take a good look.

Will lifts his arms. Hug, he says.

Martin's arms dangle uselessly by his sides. His big head droops. Hug, he says.

Martin attempts to sleep on the plane. He attempts to dream. No luck.

Or is it his luck? Lifelong, sheer and dumb. Otherwise what blooming traces might he behold? Theme-and-variation, genetic-code shebangs coursing through his brain in unruly metaphors, an ungovernable language. Un-chartable as an eerie, furling landscape through which to wander making choices determined by what our great-great-grandmothers and her forbears and offspring ate for breakfast. And that's just life, folks, Martin imagines some chipper narrator summing up. All we are, all we do, and then—where were we? we think, Martin thinks. Where was I even and who am I?

Fuck dreams, he thinks.

At his Atlanta wedding four years ago, Will and his Delaware lawyer family—mother, father, older brother, plus a distinguished-looking grandmother with a PhD in education and aunts and uncles and cousins with various educational and cultural and business pedigrees, and interesting-seeming spouses and whatnots, the whole clan Martin was aware he was romancing—met Martin's mother for the first time, at a smart downtown bistro. Apple didn't fall far from the tree. My goodness he takes after you. Martin winced through what he hoped were obligatory remarks meant kindly and watched his mother—large and awkward in an uncharacteristic cream-coloured skirt suit, her mane tamped with a taupe ribbon tied in back—fumble through the introductions. She looked pastier than usual, less tall and broad shouldered than when Martin was growing up. She seemed uncertain of herself, surrounded by Will's elegant and accomplished family. Martin tried not to feel ashamed of her, even as he pushed his own shoulders back, trying on the posture of Will's people. Even when she pursed her lips in distaste after a sip of champagne during the pre-nup toasts and Martin carefully arranged his own lips in a self-satisfied smile.

Leaving the restaurant at evening's end she sprang a lengthy bear hug on Will, who of course dealt beautifully. She caught up his hands in hers and shook them. Welcome, she said. Welcome, Will. I know Martin loves you very much.

How does she know? Martin instantly wondered. A rancid irritation writhed in him at her smugness. And welcome to what? he wondered later that night in the fancy hotel-room bed, he and Will swiping through photos of the evening on their phones. To what was she welcoming Will that she had a right to welcome him to? The so-called and much-abbreviated family?

This one's great, Will had said, stopping at a full-body image of Martin's mother, holding it up so he could see. The photo caught at Martin's throat. Couldn't Will see it too? Her shapelessness as she stood aloof from the other guests. Her superior, estranging smile which she'd regained over the course of the evening. Her self sabotaging. Her resulting loneliness. Like Martin's when he was growing up.

He'd fixed that problem, though. Here he was with

Will. Proof. Martin was not his mother. He'd made sure to not stand alone with her at the reception, to not look as if they were the odd couple out. To not stand alone period.

There she is, Will said. The proud mom you've been hiding from me. What's her story, anyway?

You have no idea, Martin said, swiping faster.

Will laughed. I don't, he said, because you never tell me. From what I saw earlier tonight, she seemed nice. Maybe a little sad.

Ha, Martin said and placed his phone on the nightstand. He turned off his bedside lamp and lay facing away. Only after a pause did he say, I'm sorry.

Another pause and Will said, That's a start.

What *is* her story? Where to truly begin?

Martin is in his mother's storage unit—the existence of which she confessed to Will during his visit with her, when she also magically bestowed the key to the unit upon him. The unit is in Blue Island, a working-class, industrial South Side Chicago neighbourhood Martin can't imagine his mother ever visiting. He sped here in his rental direct from Midway, having decided he'd deal later with the enigma that is his mother. Deal IRL or from the safety of Atlanta? he'd decided to decide later, despite what he'd told Will.

And what's with all this shit in here? Layers of totes, cardboard and plastic, and giant overstuffed trash bags that obscure the cement floor and stack up against the corrugated walls.

Some of the stuff is Martin's. He's surprised at his relief and also sickened by it. He wants to not feel a thing as he rips the tops of boxes stuffed with 'reflections' and 'research papers' he wrote in grade school and digs through old photos of himself as a miserable big-boy posed awkwardly on a rock at Promontory Point. The boy's expression says, I'd rather be at my computer, among my ribbons and trophies from science fairs—which Martin now also locates. Plus a pair of polka-dotted swim trunks he can't recall ever sporting and a few XL tees he unfortunately does remember wearing and then immediately regrets feeling badly about. When will his self-fat-shaming end and he can begin to love his formerly ample self? One of the never-ending questions. More work to do, he thinks wearily, and sifts through brown-paper bags of his old *National G*s, *Scientific American*. Hard fucking work—he can feel the dirty nails grub through his skull as the stinker viciously grasps at Martin's adult brain. If he could somehow seize the monstrous wretch and uproot him, would that boy—the unhappy flesh self—finally die? Die, Martin says aloud. Loudly? He just knows he yearns to kill the fucker, to just kill. Die, I'm begging you, Martin says for good measure.

He heaves a sigh. Off to a great start with the self love, he thinks. And what would Will, generous as he is, think of such internal violence toward this child Martin once was? Would Will still want Martin to sign on as co-parent, trust him to love another child? Would Will want Martin period? Could Martin trust himself as parent?

He staggers through more piles of lost, dubious treasures. Against all un-hoping he uncovers stacks of his mother's belongings. Unopened packs of Post-its. Clothing still in plastic wrapping, never worn. In a folded suit bag, the cream-coloured get-up she donned for his wedding. He fears the easement garbage is here too, squirreled in these blimp-like garbage bags. Proof of something only she can name or maybe can't, maybe never could—as if the bags might contain her secrets. Which are non-secrets. Symptoms of a decrepit, corrupted code, and hope to fuck it's not one he shares. A treacherous cache at the heart of the secret map stored in his own cracked cells.

Such as—paranoia, early dementia. A rotten, causative solitude.

How early, how far back did it go—might it go—before clearly manifesting?

For here there be monsters, Martin thinks, struggling for breath. For fucking real.

He can't find his old posters.

Now something assumes mass and throbs inside him. He struggles, does he ever. DUMB FUCK, Martin thinks, wiping sweat from his brow with a wadded tissue from his pants pocket. LET GO NOW.

He gingerly prods at his first pair of ice skates.

The yellowed-now kippa from his bar mitzvah, which he refused to allow the deadbeat to attend—the dad who'd proposed performing blues versions of Leonard Cohen songs during the service.

A hand-bound writing journal lovely with a repeating pattern of pomegranates on the cover. The cream-coloured inner pages are a thick, superior stock. *Italia* is embossed on the back cover. A memento, Martin guesses, of the time his mother once spent alone in Venice, away from an already wandering husband and endless arguments in a cramped apartment. Her one overseas trip, a splash-out before she started med school. Not alone—she was pregnant with Martin. When he was young she liked to talk about which churches she'd visited, the Jewish ghetto, the ducal palace. Dainty women in exquisite knits. How she found traces of her and Martin's distant ancestors after searching the ancient registers in the splendid Venetian municipal offices—how hot it was there amid the dust and declining light of late afternoon. The cool silence. The abiding waters of the canals on her solitary strolls back to her cheap hotel room.

She'd never gone anywhere after that trip. Too busy studying and then practicing medicine. Scrimping and raising Martin.

He flips the pages of the journal. All blank.

He lies down. Floating atop the sea of trash bags, the back of his neck itching from the plastic, he senses bumps and bulges clamoring distantly beneath him.

DUMB FUCK, he thinks. Maybe the story is love.

In six months, a year—however long—he'll move his mother to a nice nursing home here in Chicago. Round the clock care as needed. He and Will can afford it. Much better than moving her to Atlanta, into the house where she might mess up the baby. Maybe the baby.

Martin finishes up. Homeward fucking bound. Time to own it. Head-on face the fight of his dumb-luck life.

Alice in the Field

After, we exited the mountain. Fog grizzled the road. The tins on our backs clapped. Semi-blind we bore it all and at the bend we slowed then crossed the river. On its far bank, Pretty and Pitou straightened their skirts. Pretty had lost her shoes.

We rested, ate. First swallow, last swallow—nothing in between. A2 was there, still with us. A too. Together we bowed.

How convey such love?

I stood and smoothed my own skirt. I rummaged in my sack. Observed to myself that my instrument needed polishing.

We moved on.

That night we lit a fire and toasted Pretty's tattered right foot.

Even now these tastes come and go like glimpses of a place where peoples parade in furs. Their boat decks are broad.

Oars narrow, with blades fine as the facets of a diamond engineered without lust or greed.

All this is maintained in the literature.

What is not, is what follows.

We wept and laughed. We heaped kindling and blankets and precious warm clothes and bonfired under stars. M and A thumped stumps. We cooed. Days we traveled forests reserving tears like tar—for Small Dolly nailed to a charred oak, large Dolly spiked on a scorched pine. Stoned flat on a narrow pass, Dolly In-Between.

A Great Lake later, we roasted M's heart.

The day came when I alone straightened my skirt.

Next, the next mountain.

On a rare bluebell morning I returned alone to the valley. Stopped to rest by a low rock wall. Had lost my own shoes. Dug in my sack. My instrument required outright replacing.

I rose and resumed my walk, led by faint then louder sounds of piping, timbrels. Soon I attained a cold green meadow. Youthful limbs tangled in sinuous dance. Clusters of long-breasted grey heads chatted. Sparse-beards poked forefingers to ears and grinned at the clear sky.

Bitterness swept my blood. I shook out my uncut hair. I shut my eyes the better to see.

Snakes, I shouted. Stones that glow and stinging crawlers. Fine houses once patrolled by peacocks now vermin-run.

The music skittled to a halt. I farted and took the opportunity to cheat a glance. Of all I've seen, nothing has ever scared me so much.

I skirted a path that led to the village and in the village I found a church. That's where I stole the car.

I drove, dread in me like a wrinkled balloon. Wednesday Seventh Month. Friday Year Ten. I can report gas stations closed. Brisk trades in underpasses. More mountains filled with fog. Too dangerous to stop. To miss you all like crazy.

Sallowday Eighth. This snow. This wind.

I met Rose. Where. Swooped out of nowhere on a steep curve. Leave it at that. Hailed from the Six Cavalcades whereas the Various Eastnesses begat me. *Rose.* We camped in abandoned mansions. We pushed memories of cake between each other's sharp teeth.

Rose.

We also talked. I missed Pretty and A and A2 and the others as well and the missing was a gear grinding in my throat.

Yes, Rose would respond, folding her long skinny arms around herself, soft mouth curved like a beak. Oh yes. Mother's rape occurred on a train. Old St. John to Near Halifax, crossing the river valley. Years later, in a hospital in Lower Montreal, dying, my mother stretched her arms, reaching repeatedly in the air, thinking she was back on that train.

Dear Rose.

I know, she'd say, and crush my hand in hers. That fucking train.

And so the time came when I left Rose or she left me—no brainers. Always the fog. Always such snow. Until—solo again—I came down from the passes to a rotting village and breasts bound fathered twin dogs. Smoke and Smoke. They passed. And I in silence passed of a sort too.

Ninth Moonist Year. Found a horse, rode hard, call me lucky. On the high plains, where nineteen types of grasses rippled in the ninety winds, what was in my heart cried, but my mouth slept. I took Farther North. Spring came late then later. I moved into a crumbling apartment complex on the outskirts of a brand-spanking empty airport god-huge for what reasons I couldn't, just couldn't. I wandered the ancient buildings. I fixed the leaking pipes. I maintained the cranky boilers. Pushed mop and broom and pinched filters from cigarettes. Nights, Rose floated through my locked apartment door, locked bedroom door, bathroom door, exposing her grin and slow tremble—in this way I knew the even worse.

She was paler now of course. Under-bite more pronounced. Her, not-her. Wouldn't show those strong hands, kept them behind her skinny back.

The Ten Longest Months over, I stood outside the complex in a fair rain. I'd washed and ironed my skirt. Donned a cape of blanket and plastic sheeting.

For a few seconds, in grey sequins that matched the mist, M and Pitou paraded across the vacant lot adjacent my building. They vanished with no trace.

Rose joined by A2 and Pretty flickered at my old apartment window.

I left before they went out.

Peoples with shivering scales for lips and a scorpion-spider bucked onto the page of a book a daughter reads on the back deck of her house in New Richmond. A green sky stretches around her and turns tangerine.

Someone's mother's beloved Montserrat under ash.

Someone's mother's fox-thrice-played-with in the weeds blooming by a house on a hill in Old-Timey Rothesay. River town, river smell.

Silent forms.

Equatorial nights bring Ophiuchus, Serpentarius, Aesclepius the healer, the thirteenth, exile.

I arrive. At long last. Snow falls in the mountains, Argentina.

For you, darlings, were loveliest of them all.

Acknowledgements

These stories appeared, in often different form, in the following: "Money's Honey" in *The New Quarterly*; "The Riddles of Aramaic" in *The Malahat Review*; "Armada" in *Sententia*, *16: Best Canadian Stories*, and in very different form in the novel *Blue Field*; "Made Right Here" in *The Gettysburg Review*; "All We Did" in *Gargoyle*; "Public Storage Available Now" in *PANK*; "This Wicked Tongue" in *The Walrus*; "Princess Gates" in *Bateau*; "Alice in the Field," a finalist for *The Best Small Fictions 2018*, in *The Collagist*.

Many thanks to Jessica Johnson, Mark Drew, Richard Peabody, Jen Michalski, John Barton, and Gabriel Blackwell. My profound gratitude to John Metcalf, keeper of the faith. Thank you as well to Dan Wells, Vanessa Stauffer, Casey Plett, Chris Andrechek. Thanks and love to David Smooke and Michael Kimball, to Joel Levine, and to Susie Brandt, Regina DeLuise, Katherine Kavanaugh, Tom Livingston, Sherrie Flick.

I'm grateful as well to Cyndy Hayward and the Willapa Bay AiR for providing time and space during which some of these stories were written.

Elise Levine is the author of two novels, *Blue Field* and *Requests and Dedications*, and the story collection *Driving Men Mad*. Her work has also appeared in *Ploughshares*, *The Gettysburg Review*, *The Collagist*, *Blackbird*, *Best Canadian Stories*, and the *Journey Prize Anthology*, among other publications, and was named a finalist for *The Best Small Fictions 2018*. She has taught creative writing at Johns Hopkins University and American University, and lives in Baltimore, MD.